Stranded on the Beach

Holiday Acres, Book One

NOELLE ADAMS

Holiday Acres

Stranded on the Beach (Phil and Rebecca)

Stranded in the Snow (Scott and Olivia)

Stranded in the Woods (Kent and Penny)

Stranded for Christmas (Russ and Laura)

One

On a different day, Rebecca Holiday might have thought being forced to take a two-week vacation at the beach was a pretty good problem to have, but today she wasn't happy about it.

In fact, she was having trouble not scowling as her sister showed her around the lovely beach house her family had rented for her on the Eastern Shore of Virginia.

"Laura," Rebecca said, trying to get her sister's attention.

At thirty-one years old, Laura was the oldest of the four Holiday sisters, and she'd been bossy and driven all her life. She wasn't easily swayed from her mission as she opened doors and blinds and sometimes drawers on her tour of the house, showing off the three large bedrooms, updated fixtures, and expansive bay views.

Rebecca loved the house—especially the sunlight streaming in through the wide windows, the covered patio with a porch swing, and the luxurious master bathroom. But when Laura told her this morning that her sisters had arranged a surprise for her twenty-fifth birthday, Rebecca hadn't expected to drive three hours across Virginia and then be informed she was being left here on her own for two weeks.

"Laura, wait," she tried again.

Laura was pretty in a no-nonsense way with brown hair, brown eyes, freckles, and a slim figure. She always walked quickly, particularly when she was excited about something. At the moment, she was speed-walking down the long hallway of the main level—the second floor of the house—to take advantage of the water views over the dunes.

When her sister kept going, Rebecca raised her voice. "Laura!"

Stopping abruptly and turning around, Laura asked, "What's the matter? Don't you like it?"

"Yes, I like it. It's amazing. But I don't understand what's happening here."

"What's happening is that we all chipped in and arranged this vacation for you."

"But why?" Rebecca's voice cracked slightly. From bewilderment, disorientation, and some sort of deeper emotion.

"Because you need it." Laura said the words as if they were obvious, as if that was the only answer Rebecca needed.

It wasn't.

"I do not need it. Not any more than anyone else. Why would you all—"

"You *do* need it." Laura's expression softened slightly as she stepped closer to Rebecca. "We all know you need it. You've been exhausted lately, and you refuse to take any downtime."

"I don't need—"

"Yes, you do. Stop saying you don't. You passed out last week and ended up in the emergency room, didn't you?"

Rebecca made a dismissive gesture with her hand. "That's because I'd gone all day without eating. You know how stressed I was, getting ready for Charlotte's wedding.

That woman was a bridezilla if there ever was one. But it's over now. We don't have any more events like that coming up. I'm not going to forget to eat again, and it's—"

"It's not just occasionally forgetting to eat. You've lost weight. You're always tired. You don't swim or jog anymore. You're worn out. Even the doctor said so. You took care of Mom all last year, and you never took any time to recover after she died."

"All of us—"

"We all did what we could, but you did the most. Don't try to deny it."

Rebecca couldn't deny it. She had been their mother's primary caretaker for more than a year after she was diagnosed with cancer, suffered through a number of treatments, and then finally died almost six months ago. Her sisters all had much more essential roles in the family business than she did, and taking care of sick people was something Rebecca was good at.

She'd been so glad to be able to take care of her mother in the last year of her life, but it had been hard. Really hard.

Although she wasn't about to admit the truth to Laura, she was still exhausted from the physical and emotional strain.

Laura was still talking. "And now, on top of everything else you do, you take care of Tommy every day."

Tommy was Laura's six-year-old son, the consequence of a one-night stand with an asshole who'd never even wanted to meet his son. Since Laura was so busy with responsibilities in the family business, Rebecca had started looking after her nephew when he wasn't in school.

"Taking care of Tommy isn't a burden. You know I love him."

"I know you do. And we love you. You refuse to take days off when we ask you to, and you're just getting more and more tired. So we had to take drastic measures to get you to take some time off."

"It's not that bad." Rebecca understood what was happening now, but she was still disoriented by the unexpectedness. She felt almost dizzy and wished she could sit down. "All of us work hard. We have to."

She was convinced she didn't work any harder than her sisters did. They all had different gifts, and so they'd taken on different responsibilities.

Thirty years ago, their father, Jed Holiday, had bought a large piece of land outside Charlottesville, Virginia, and had opened a Christmas tree farm.

His trees had been highly sought after, and he'd slowly grown a wider business to go along with the farm that included cozy, picturesque cottages for vacation rentals, a coffee shop and bakery, a quaint barn and gardens for events, and a Christmas shop so large that people would drive hours to visit. Holiday Acres had been a thriving business when their father died five years ago, and his wife and daughters had kept expanding it ever since.

Laura handled the business and financial side of things with her characteristic efficiency.

Penny, the second oldest and artistic by nature, oversaw anything creative or aesthetic connected with Holiday Acres.

Olivia, two years older than Rebecca, dealt with all the public relations because she was so good with people.

And that left Rebecca with whatever remained to be done behind the scenes.

She didn't mind. She wasn't as brilliant and talented as her sisters. She still loved Holiday Acres, and she wanted to help however she could. The only task she really hated was running herself ragged assisting spoiled, demanding brides who were getting married in their event spaces.

"I know we all work hard," Laura was saying now. "No one is denying that. But what you've had to do—particularly with Mom—took a lot out of you, and we're worried about you."

"I'm fi—"

"Don't try to tell me you're fine. You're exhausted. When was the last time you tried to cook? You love cooking, and I can't remember the last time you've done it just for fun. You don't hang out with your friends as much as you used to. And you haven't been on a date in more than a year."

"There's not been anyone I've wanted to date."

"Maybe. Maybe not. But it's more than that, and you know it. We want to do something for you, and this is what we're going to do. So stop whining about a vacation and just deal with it."

Rebecca made a face at her sister's tone, but she didn't want to seem ungrateful, so she relaxed intentionally. "Okay. Fine. I don't mind taking a few days' vacation. But two weeks is too long."

"No, it's not. It's the right amount of time since it's going to take you a few days to even wind down so you can rest. We thought we'd get you a place here because the ocean beaches are always so packed and chaotic this time of year. It's quieter here. Not so frantic. We've stocked the refrigerator and the pantry so you have plenty of food. You can cook to your heart's content. And you saw that grocery store we passed down the road, so you can get more stuff if you need it. There are several little restaurants within fairly easy walking distance if you go into town, so you don't even have to cook if you don't want." As she talked, Laura walked into the kitchen where she opened a small drawer. "You've got plenty of cash here for anything you need."

"I don't need cash."

"Yes, you do, because I've got your wallet and I'm not giving it back."

"*What?*" Rebecca's voice was suddenly louder than before.

"I don't trust you not to rent a car and just come back home if you have access to a credit card."

"But I've got to have a car."

"No, you don't. What do you need a car for? You're going to be taking it easy for the next two weeks. We've loaded up your Kindle with books, and I've set you up with every streaming service known to man so you can watch anything you want on TV. You've got a pool and hot tub at this house, and the beach is right there, and you can walk to any store or restaurant you want in town. You're not getting a car."

"But I'll be... I'll be stranded here!"

Laura nodded. "Exactly right. You're going to have a good time and relax even if we have to force it on you."

"But Laura..." For once, Rebecca wasn't interrupted. She trailed off, her mind whirling with what was happening.

"But nothing." Laura's expression changed as she closed the drawer with all the cash in it. "Rebecca, you've taken care of people all your life, and you never ask for anything in return. You gave Mom everything she needed last year when none of the rest of us could have done it. You take care of my son every single day, and I can't begin to tell you how grateful I am for that. You don't take days off. You don't do anything for yourself. You're like Beth from freaking

Little Women, and we're not going to let you waste away like she did."

Rebecca's eyes blurred, and her throat ached with a wave of unexpected emotion. "Don't make it sound like I'm a martyr. I just… just do what I'm good at. Like we all do."

"I know that. But what you do is important. And it's hard. It's *hard*. Maybe you think no one really notices, but we do. We notice. We see you. We love you. And we want to do this for you. Please let us."

Rebecca swallowed hard and gave a mute nod.

Laura's posture relaxed, and she reached into her bag for a small flip phone. "Okay then. You need to hold on to this so you have a phone in case of emergency or if you want to talk to us just to chat."

"What? Why do I need this archaic piece of junk? It's not even a smartphone."

"Of course it's not. You need to relax—not spend all day messing around on email and your phone." When Rebecca started to ask a question, Laura gave her a flash of a smile. "Oh, didn't I tell you? I'm not just taking your wallet. I'm also taking your phone."

~

That evening, Rebecca took a walk on the beach. She'd spent the afternoon getting acclimated to the house and her situation, and it was harder than one would think to be without all the normal accoutrements of modern life like a phone, a car, and a credit card.

It was also hard and strange to be so entirely alone.

She'd been in college getting a degree in elementary education when her father died. She'd never felt a strong urge to be a teacher, but she loved children and it seemed like a natural fit.

What she'd really wanted to do was get married, have children, and raise a family, but that felt like a risky thing to admit in a family as dynamic and ambitious as hers was. Plus the one guy she'd ever really wanted for a husband had dumped her in the most painful of ways. No matter how much she told herself to grow up, get over it, and find someone else, no one else had yet been able to equal his memory.

She'd never gotten a teaching job after she graduated. They'd needed her at home, and she was happy working at Holiday Acres with her family.

Maybe she was a little tired lately, but she didn't need this crazy vacation dropped in her lap.

The house was gorgeous but strangely silent after the constant activity at home, and it was odd not to have Tommy hanging around all the time with his pesky questions and loud laughter and sweet hugs.

She missed him. And she missed her sisters. And she missed the staff, all of whom she considered her friends.

What the hell was she supposed to do by herself for two weeks?

She told herself that if it was too lonely and boring, she'd call up Laura and demand that someone come and get her. But she didn't want to do that unless she had to because it was clear her sisters were really trying to do something nice for her.

She did appreciate it.

She just wished they'd chosen to make a different gesture of affection than this.

She walked a long time—a few miles on the beach along the Chesapeake Bay—because she was so restless and at loose ends, and the sun was getting lower in the sky when she returned and approached her house.

There were homes spread out along the shoreline, but every square foot wasn't crammed with huge vacation rentals and condos like on the ocean beaches. Some of the houses were privately owned, and some were rented out. Some were huge, and some, like hers, were smaller, intimate. She'd run into some people on the beach but not any huge crowds.

If she'd had to be stranded on a beach by herself, she could have done a lot worse than this.

There was a fishing pier not far from her house, extending out into the bay and connected to a little shop and seafood restaurant. The breeze was warm and pleasant, and she didn't want to go sit by herself in the house quite yet, so she bought an ice-cream cone from the shop, walked out on the pier, and sat down on a bench at the end of it.

The sun would be setting soon. She'd stay here until the light was gone, and then she'd go back home, take a soak in the hot tub, and go to bed early.

She was tired.

Maybe she was more tired than she'd thought.

She wasn't used to being all alone with just her own thoughts for company.

How had she ended up here?

Just this morning, she'd woken up expecting it to be a normal day.

She sat for about twenty minutes, feeling the breeze and the lowering sun on her skin.

She'd passed a few people fishing in the middle of the pier, but there was no one right where she was. Not until a man walked by her just then with a fishing pole and a tackle bag.

She hadn't been looking when he approached and walked past her, so she only saw him from the back. He was young—she could tell even without seeing his face. He had a lean, upright figure, nice shoulders, and a tight butt beneath his cargo shorts. His too-long hair was golden brown, glinting in the light of the sun.

She watched him idly since there was nothing else to watch.

She didn't know for sure, but she guessed he would be very good-looking when she saw his face.

He found his spot at the railing of the pier, put down his bag, and cast his rod.

Rebecca wondered if she would like to fish. She'd never done it before. It seemed like a pleasant, peaceful activity. Maybe a little boring.

If she ran out of things to do, maybe she would try it.

She watched the guy fish for a while, but he didn't turn to look at her or even glance in her direction. She only saw his back. It was a very fine back, but it was unsettling that he was so completely oblivious to her presence.

She wasn't a take-charge person like Laura or the life of the party like Olivia. She didn't even have a unique, whimsical personality and sense of style like Penny.

Rebecca was pretty enough with hair a lighter brown than her sisters, a compact figure, and blue eyes that were a little too big for her face. Today she wore a pair of brown shorts, a fitted white T-shirt, and walking sandals. She was used to fading into the background, but she wasn't used to being invisible.

She might not have been in the dating mood lately, but some guys liked how she looked. Some guys noticed her.

She had the strange impulse to say something, make a noise, bang her feet on the pier—just to get the man's attention.

It was silly and immature, so she didn't indulge the impulse. He was obviously lost in his own thoughts and didn't care about a stray woman who happened to be sitting on the pier where he fished.

She did like the looks of his back. She'd always liked men shaped like him—fit in a lean way rather than bulky. He was probably no more than four inches taller than her own five six. She could see muscles rippling beneath the thin fabric of his white T-shirt as he moved, but they were natural, graceful. Not overblown.

And he had a really great butt.

She hadn't seen such a great butt on a man since…

She wasn't going to think about him.

It had been almost seven years now since Phil Matheson had dumped her, and she was still trying not to think about him.

With a sigh, she stood up and turned to walk away.

She was supposed to be on vacation. To get rest. To feel better. Mooning over the boy who hadn't wanted her enough to stay wasn't the way to do that.

A gust of wind picked up just then and whipped her hair back. She had it tied loosely with a scarf, but the scarf got caught in the breeze and blew right out of her hair.

"Damn it," she muttered, when she made a grab for it and missed. It kept blowing over toward the silent man, still fishing.

He turned around just in time to snatch the scarf as it blew toward him.

She was about to give him an automatic thank-you, but the words died on her lips.

This man didn't just remind her of Phil Matheson from the back.

This man *was* Phil Matheson.

With his amber brown eyes and his high cheekbones and the little cleft in his chin.

Phil.

Standing right there in front of her.

Her mouth dropped open as she froze. She had no idea how this was happening. Phil had walked out on her—on his family, on everyone—when he was just nineteen. His father and her father had gotten into a huge fight that had led to a bitter feud that couldn't be resolved. Their entire community had been pulled into the conflict, everyone taking sides, and the friendships the girls had always had with the Matheson boys had been irrevocably torn apart.

It had been worse for Rebecca and Phil. They'd been a lot more than friends.

Rebecca had thought they were in love. Whatever Phil had felt for her, however, hadn't been strong enough to withstand their families' conflict. They'd broken up, and he'd moved out of town for good. When their fathers died two years later—both men died in the same tragic accident—Phil had come back for two days for the funeral. He hadn't even spoken to her, and she hadn't seen him since.

When the truth about the feud finally came out a few years ago, Rebecca had been heartbroken to discover that her father had been mostly to blame. He'd made some bad mistakes. He'd hurt a lot of people—including Phil's family.

So Rebecca couldn't blame Phil for resenting her father. But she hadn't been to blame. She hadn't even known what her father had done. And Phil had still walked out on her and everyone else in his life, offering her nothing but an impossible choice if she'd wanted them to stay together.

She hadn't deserved that.

A long time ago, she'd figured out the truth. The only answer that made sense of his leaving. Phil hadn't loved her the way she'd loved him. And he hadn't been the man she'd believed him to be if he could leave everyone important to him behind and never look back.

She'd had no idea where he'd been all these years, but evidently he had been here.

On the Eastern Shore. On a fishing pier just before sunset.

He was holding her scarf in his hands and staring at her in a daze.

He was just as shocked to see her as she was to see him.

All her old feelings for him had risen up in a rush, making her chest hurt, making her breathing ragged. She put a hand over her heart and tried to make her voice work.

Phil managed before she did. "What are you doing here?" he demanded.

She just stared at him. Confused by his tone. Confused by everything.

"I asked you what you're doing here." He sounded angry.

Angry.

At her.

Everyone who knew Rebecca would testify that she was a nice person by nature. People called her sweet. Gentle.

A girl in high school who'd been jealous of Rebecca's dating Phil had always called her spineless.

But she wasn't spineless, and his resentful tone hit her hard, rousing a long-sleeping wave of indignation.

"What am I doing here? What do you think? I'm on vacation, and this is a public pier. I'm not trespassing on your private property."

His eyes were searching her face with a strange urgency, but he held on to his scowl. "But why here?"

"Why—" She cut off the words as she realized what he was implying. What he thought. She clenched her hands at her sides. "I didn't come here on purpose to stalk you, if that's what you're thinking. I had no idea where you were. You dropped off the planet as far as everyone back home is concerned. And if I'd known you were here, I would have stayed as far away as possible."

His eyes narrowed. The sun was very low now, casting streams of orange light onto the water, onto the pier, onto Phil's tanned skin and golden hair. For a moment he was so stunningly handsome she couldn't take a full breath. "Then how did you end up here?" he asked, that same implied accusation in his tone.

If she'd been a violent person, she might have slapped him or scratched his eyes out. She'd never been violent. She'd never even been loud. But she'd also rarely been as angry as she was now.

She'd never done anything bad to Phil. *Anything.* She'd only ever loved him. Her father had hurt his family, and she could understand lingering bitterness. But he shouldn't blame her for what her father had done.

He shouldn't, but evidently he did.

"I told you. I'm on vacation. You're the last person in the world I ever expected to see here. I don't care if you believe me or not. It's a good thing I didn't come here wanting to find you," she said, her voice so cool it was almost unrecognizable. "Because if I had, I'd have had to admit defeat. There's obviously nothing of who you used to be left in who you are now."

She was almost shocked at herself for the lucid and cutting retort, and she punctuated it by turning her back to him and walking away.

She moved quickly, but he wasn't trying to follow her.

He'd actually believed she'd come here on purpose to hook up with him again.

The idea mortified and infuriated her, and it couldn't be further from the truth.

He'd always been kind and good-natured—at least she'd always thought he was. They'd started dating when she was sixteen and he was seventeen. She'd known him all her life, but she'd always only thought of him as the son of her father's friend until that year in high school. He'd started to talk to her at lunch period and after school. He'd had this sweet, funny way of approaching her, as if he thought she was special but didn't want to make a big deal about it. He'd made her laugh. He'd really seemed to listen when she talked. He'd loved all the food she cooked for him. They'd dated until the summer after she'd graduated high school. She'd been dreaming of his proposing after a year or two of college, but then everything fell apart.

He obviously wasn't the same person anymore.

Neither was she.

She might still be quiet, but she wasn't a pushover. And she wasn't going to let him make her feel bad about herself.

She returned to her beach house, and the first thing she did was call up her sister on the stupid flip phone she'd been given for emergencies.

This definitely counted as an emergency.

Laura picked up with a friendly greeting.

Rebecca was almost growling as she said, "Damn it, Laura. You did this on purpose."

Two

Phil Matheson filled up a travel mug with coffee the next morning and was walking out the door when he paused next to his old pine dresser.

He picked up a soft blue scarf and fingered it idly.

There was no reason for him to have held on to it. It obviously wasn't expensive, and Rebecca wasn't likely to ever ask for it back. But after he'd caught it blowing in the wind on the pier yesterday, he'd brought it with him and laid it down on his dresser.

What the hell was she doing here?

And why did she have to still be so gorgeous, so full of a hidden fire he'd always sensed beneath her mild surface.

He'd known that fire was there back in high school, even though the rest of the town had assumed she was nothing but sweet and quiet. He'd felt something warm, life-giving, compelling in her, and he'd intentionally pursued it.

Seven years had passed now. More than enough time for him to forget her, move on, find something else to fill his heart and mind.

But the moment he'd seen her again, standing on the pier in her shorts and windblown hair, he'd seen, known, experienced all that old fire again.

And he'd wanted it as much as he had before.

It was honestly a little annoying.

He'd created a new life for himself. It was his. The bay, the quiet beach, the quaint towns, the slow rhythm of days here on the Eastern Shore.

They were *his*.

If he'd wanted to be reminded of his previous life and get slammed with all these old feelings, he could have gone back home. His past and all he'd left behind weren't supposed to materialize in front of him one evening in the form of one small pretty blonde.

He dropped the scarf back on the dresser and walked outside. He'd lived in this run-down studio apartment since he'd moved to town seven years ago. It was the second floor of a small building on the outskirts of town. Beneath him was a storage unit the owner used for boating and beach equipment, and out the west-facing windows he could see the Chesapeake Bay.

He rode his bike into town and ended up at the seafood restaurant and fishing shop he co-owned with a friend. He'd stumbled into the business five years ago the way he stumbled through life now. The opportunity had fallen into his lap. His friend Larry was responsible for the restaurant and all the financial aspects of the business. All Phil had to bring was his expertise in fishing and some basic skills in sales.

Mostly he just hung around, talking to tourists and locals about fishing and occasionally giving private lessons.

He wasn't ever going to get rich doing this, but he didn't want to get rich.

He just wanted to live his life without hurting again, trying too much, feeling too deeply.

He'd managed.

For a lot of years, he'd managed.

And he would keep managing as long as Rebecca didn't show up in his world again.

What the *hell* was she doing here?

It wasn't even seven in the morning yet when he opened the shop and got out his fishing gear. In the mornings, he had to staff the store so he couldn't go all the way out on the pier. He greeted a couple of retired guys who came every morning to fish, and then he took a position on the pier close enough to get back to the shop if a customer happened to stop in.

The few expensive fishing rods he kept were all locked behind glass, and the chance of being robbed for some tackle or bait was negligible.

As he cast his line, he wondered if Rebecca would appear again this evening.

She'd said she was renting a house nearby.

It was too big a coincidence to believe, but she'd clearly been as shocked as he had yesterday. She hadn't known he was living here.

Someone else must be responsible for her presence here.

~

The morning was already hot and humid—too muggy for this early in the summer—and Phil was sweating a half hour later when he went back to the shop to fill up his travel mug with more coffee.

He stopped for a few minutes to chat with old Carl Henner, who'd moved to town when he retired and hung out at local businesses most of the day.

He was returning to the pier with his coffee when he jerked to a stop.

Rebecca. Standing no more than ten feet away from him. Her back was to him as she snapped a few photos of the bay with her phone. She wore another pair of shorts that made the most of her firm, round ass and tanned legs. Her hair was in a ponytail, tied with an elastic thing today rather than a scarf.

Every muscle in his body tightened at the sight of her. His heart started to hammer in his chest.

She lowered her phone and turned around, jerking to a stop exactly as he had earlier when her eyes landed on him.

They stared at each other for a long moment, and Phil tried to fight a pull in the vicinity of his chest, some kind of compulsion that dragged him toward her.

"I thought you came here in the evenings," she said at last. Her voice wasn't loud, but there was an edge of both resentment and defensiveness in it that immediately raised Phil's hackles.

"You really assume I keep the exact same schedule every day?" He did, but there was no way she could know that.

"I don't know. Why are you here again?"

He frowned as he stepped closer. "I don't have to justify my presence to you. I've been here a lot longer than you. This is where I live."

"I'm not expecting you to justify anything to me." She was angry now too. Her cheeks were flushed and her eyes flashing. "I just wondered if you really hung around fishing all day long like an old man."

"Hanging around fishing is my job. I co-own that store and restaurant." He nodded back toward the shop, pleased he had something to show for the years they'd been apart.

She blinked, some of her anger fading in her surprise. She'd always been like that. She wasn't an angry person. It took a lot to rile her up, and even then she was easily diverted by other emotions. "Really?"

"You think I'd stand here and lie to you?"

"I don't know. I don't know you anymore."

"Then there'd be no reason for me to lie to you about what I'm doing. You think I have any interest in impressing you?"

He did want to impress her. He could feel the impulse niggling in his head, even as he told himself it didn't matter at all what she thought of him.

He didn't want to feel that way though.

He didn't want to care so much about someone he'd long since left behind.

He wanted to go back to his relaxed, even-tempered life where nothing pushed him too far or went too deep or hurt him too much. He'd shaped his life that way on purpose, and he couldn't fight the swell of resentment that Rebecca had shown up out of the blue and taken it away from him.

"So you're here at the pier all day?" she asked, a different expression on her face.

He'd always been able to read her, and he could see what she was thinking right now. She was confused and disappointed and hoping for a time during the day when she could come out this way without accidentally running into him.

If he was smart, he would give her a time—any time—and then make sure he wasn't around then for the next week or two, however long she was in town. He could manage it, and it was the only way of maintaining control over his feelings.

He needed to just tell her he wasn't around at lunchtime, when he normally left to do errands or work out. Then he'd be safe. They'd avoid each other.

Lunchtime.

Tell her.

Now.

"I work here. I'm around all the time," he said.

Her mouth and jaw tightened. "Well, I'm in that house for the next two weeks." She nodded with her head toward a small, expensive vacation rental a few houses down from the pier. "When I walk, I'm going to end up here."

"You can walk in the other direction."

Her shoulders stiffened. Clearly his cold voice had angered her. "I'm allowed to walk in any direction I want. You think I'm supposed to curtail my vacation just because you happen to work here?"

"I didn't tell you to curtail anything. I merely suggested if you didn't want to see me, then you could avoid it."

"I don't want to see you."

"Then walk in the other direction."

"You asshole," she hissed. "I'm not going make things easy for you. I'll show up here whenever I want."

"And I'll be here."

"That's fine with me. I don't care enough about you to keep me from doing what I want to do."

The only time he'd ever seen her this angry was when they'd broken up. She'd been hurt—really hurt—but she'd also been furious, denouncing him for letting their families come between them and for not understanding what love really was.

Time hadn't healed over the rift for her, any more than it had for him.

"You think I do care?" he said. "You can do whatever the hell you want."

"Then I will. I'm going to come every single day."

"Fine."

"Fine." She was glaring at him, her small body tense, motionless. The sun was higher in the sky now, and it cast beams of warm light on her tanned skin, her golden hair. She glowed beautifully, vibrantly.

And Phil was hit by the strongest wave of attraction he'd ever experienced.

In his *life*.

It slammed into him, nearly knocking him off his feet. His eyes glazed over. His mind whirled. His body tensed up. His groin hardened.

There was nothing in the world he could do to stop the feeling. He wanted her so much he could barely stay on his feet.

"What's the matter with you?" Rebecca demanded.

Phil gulped, trying to pull himself together. He couldn't let her see, let her know. That would be a humiliation too far. Acutely aware of the fact that he was more than halfway erect—from nothing more than that irrational attraction—he shifted from foot to foot and tried to breathe out his physical response. "Nothing's wrong with me."

"Then why do you look like you've been punched in the gut?" Her eyes were scanning his face and body now.

It wouldn't take her long to figure it out.

He scowled at her and made himself move, walking away from her quickly, toward the pier, without saying anything else.

"I'm not going to stay away," she called out to his back.

"I don't give a damn what you do."

He was satisfied that he sounded bad-tempered but not overwhelmed with lust. He took his position again and exhaled deeply when he saw her striding away, continuing the walk she'd started earlier.

This wasn't good.

It wasn't good at all.

She was evidently going to be here for two weeks. And she wasn't going to stay away from the pier.

He was going to have to see her again. Maybe a lot. And he couldn't avoid her without backing down from her implicit challenge.

He wouldn't do that.

He'd left his hometown seven years ago because it was the only way he could be his own person and not a man shaped by a dysfunctional family and a history of betrayal.

He couldn't let Rebecca take that away from him now.

~

For his entire childhood, Phil's father and Rebecca's father had been best friends. The men had grown up together, and they'd both found work and raised families in their hometown. Rebecca's father had eventually made a lot of money, while Phil's father was always struggling. Phil hadn't thought it mattered. He'd been happy growing up, and their families had always been close.

Then seven years ago, Phil's father had discovered a secret that had been buried for years. Jed Holiday's business might have been successful, but it was built on a lie, on a deep betrayal.

Phil's grandfather had helped out Holiday early on and, per their verbal agreement, should have been given a piece of the business profits when Holiday Acres started to do well.

But Holiday had been a businessman more than a friend, and he'd cheated the Matheson family out of what they deserved.

Then when Phil's father had discovered this from going through papers after Phil's grandfather's death, Holiday had outright denied it.

The conflict had intensified and spread to their families—and then to the larger community, all of whom had taken sides. So many people refused to believe that Jed Holiday would cheat anyone, so the Mathesons had paid a large price for trying to seek justice and vindication.

There was no way Phil's relationship with Rebecca could survive such a thing. She kept defending her father, and Phil couldn't stomach it for long.

The feud continued until both their fathers died, but Phil left town long before then.

The conflict had knit Rebecca's family closer together, but it had torn Phil's family apart.

Four years ago, Laura Holiday had uncovered proof that the Mathesons had been right all along. Their grandfather had been cheated by Jed Holiday. Mrs. Holiday and her daughters had made a gesture of reconciliation by offering the surviving Mathesons a partnership in Holiday Acres.

Phil had refused. He wanted nothing to do with it. With them.

His two brothers had also refused. They hadn't left the area like he had, but they were just as embittered by how their family had been treated.

The only Matheson who had accepted the offer was Phil's Uncle Russ, his father's much younger brother.

Phil had been surprised by his uncle's actions, and he'd been angry at first since it offered the Holidays a way to assuage their guilt.

He was thinking about this—about all this—when his phone rang later that day and he saw his Uncle Russ's name on the screen.

Ever since he'd left town, Russ had called him once a week. Like clockwork. No matter what. Even at the beginning, when Phil hadn't even answered the phone.

He stared at the name for a few seconds before he answered. "Hey."

"Hi, Phil. How's it going?"

"Not good. But I'm guessing you know something about that."

"What do I know?" Russ was only in his midforties, but for as long as Phil could remember, Russ had acted like a cynical old man—always ironically distant, like he observed the world from outside instead of actually living it. He sounded almost amused right now with a dry irony Phil knew well.

"No one back at home knows where I am except you, Kent, and Scott. They would never have told anyone, so I'm assuming it must be you."

"Did someone you know show up unexpectedly?"

His uncle's wry amusement made him snarl. "This isn't funny. It's downright mean. Do you really hate me that much?"

"I don't hate you, Phil," Russ said, his tone changing into a rare, tired earnestness. "You know I don't. And honestly I had nothing to do with it except answering when Laura asked me where you were."

"Laura? So it was her?"

"Who else? The woman thinks she can arrange the whole world to her specifications, and most of the time she's right."

Phil paused for a moment, thinking through what he'd just heard in Russ's voice. It wasn't just the normal amused irony. There was something else there too.

Something almost fond.

"You like them," Phil said, soft and accusatory. "Damn it, Russ. You told me you joined up with them for the money, but it's more than that now. You *like* them."

Russ didn't answer immediately. "They can't be blamed for what their father did."

"But they can be blamed for what they did afterward."

"They didn't know. He was their father, and they didn't know."

"And the man they cheated was *your* father. Does that mean nothing to you?"

"Sure it does. But it's years over now. Enough damage has been done. It's not worth holding on to."

"I think you're wrong."

"Maybe. I've been wrong before."

"Damn it, Russ."

"You've said that already. A couple of times."

Phil let out a hoarse sigh. "Shit."

"Hiding out the way you've been doing obviously isn't working for you."

"It is work—"

"So maybe you could consider getting closure—with Rebecca at least. She was eighteen years old when everything happened. She was barely more than a child. You really think that sweet little girl was evil for believing her dad?"

The words stabbed Phil through the heart. Made him feel stupid, guilty. "There's more to it than that. You know that. And I never thought she was evil."

"So talk to her. Find out who she is now. Get some closure. You don't have to do anything drastic or give up your lazy life of fishing and avoiding all things personal. Just talk to her. I bet you'll find that all those memories aren't as painful afterward. It worked for me."

Phil ended the call without too much bitterness, and he thought about what Russ had said for a long time.

Closure.

It would be nice.

And it didn't have to change anything substantial in the life he'd made for himself here.

Three

That evening, Rebecca got an ice-cream cone and walked out onto the pier, knowing she'd run into Phil.

She wasn't normally like this. She usually avoided conflict when she could and didn't fight battles that would never accomplish something worthwhile. Normally, she'd tell herself it wasn't worth it and just let it go.

But she wasn't going to let Phil believe she was cowed—by him and the prospect of seeing him again. He probably still thought of her as that naïve, compliant girl he'd known from high school—one he could scare off with glowers and glares.

She wasn't that girl anymore, and she wasn't going to let him win.

So she made her way down the beach and then out on the pier, recognizing Phil's lean back at the far end in the same position he'd been the evening before. She didn't go all the way out to him, but she went far enough that it was clear she wasn't afraid of running into him.

She stood there, looking out at the sky and the bay, and she licked her chocolate ice cream as quickly as she could before it melted.

Phil didn't turn to look at her. She wasn't even sure he knew she was there.

It bothered her.

She was acutely conscious of him, but he wasn't of her.

She was trying to decide what she should do when her borrowed phone rang. She hesitated briefly before she flipped it open and answered the call.

"Are you still mad at me?" Laura asked.

"Kind of."

"I'm sorry."

"No, you're not."

"I was just trying to help. You know that."

"I know, but it doesn't make it better. I still feel used, being set up like this. And I don't know how you could possibly think it would help me. What good can come out of this ridiculous matchmaking with a guy who dumped me years ago? There's obviously no hope for a future with him now."

"Oh no," Laura said, more earnest now, worried. "I really wasn't trying to be a matchmaker. That's not me at all."

"Then why would you—"

"I thought you needed closure."

"Closure?" Rebecca nibbled at her cone and licked up some more melted ice cream. It was a race against time with it now to get it eaten before it all dribbled away.

"Yes. Closure. That's really all this was about. You needed a vacation. That much was real. Penny and Olivia thought so too, so they helped with the plans. And then I've always been worried that you're still holding on to... that you haven't moved on from him."

"I have. I have moved on."

"Have you? You haven't given another guy a second glance since high school."

"I've dated—"

"You've gone through the motions. You never considered any of those guys seriously. Be honest with yourself."

Rebecca breathed through the wave of resentment and tried to think it through sincerely.

And Laura was right.

Of course she was right.

Rebecca had never really gotten over what happened with Phil. He was always at the back of her mind whenever she dated other men.

Laura went on as if Rebecca had answered. "So I thought, why not combine a vacation with a possibility of getting closure. I'm not expecting you to run off and marry him or anything stupid like that. You know I don't believe in fated soul mates or one-true-loves or any of that nonsense. I'm practical. And, practically speaking, you need to resolve things better than they were resolved before. So I thought if you saw him again, maybe you could…"

Rebecca sighed, her eyes resting on Phil's upright back and golden brown hair. "I don't know if closure is possible."

"Of course it is. It's always possible even if it's just one-sided. Give it a chance. Talk to him. Get to know him how he is now. You'll probably realize that he's not anything like you remember, and then you'll see that you wouldn't even want him anymore. Wouldn't knowing that help you move on?"

Rebecca felt a stirring in her chest as she watched Phil with his fishing rod, a force inside her reaching for him, drawing her toward him.

She'd felt that same force when she was a teenager. She'd believed it was the most powerful feeling in the world back then.

But she was older now. Smarter. And it would be very nice to get to the point where she had that stirring force under control.

He did seem different.

Maybe Laura was right.

Maybe if she tried to see him for who he was now she would finally get rid of this compulsion toward him.

It was worth a try anyway.

"You still there?" Laura asked.

"Yeah. Sorry. Just thinking."

"Okay. I get it if you're still mad at me, but at least think about what I said. I'm usually right, you know."

Rebecca made a grumbling noise—the only fit response for Laura's claim—and then she said goodbye and hung up.

She kept gazing in Phil's direction as she finished her ice cream, and she was wiping her mouth when he suddenly turned around and looked right at her.

Their eyes met across the distance.

Closure.

It wasn't a bad idea.

She did want to be free of these feelings.

She felt herself making a strange little nod.

After a moment, Phil returned the gesture. Just a nod. Not even a smile.

But it felt like they'd understood each other. Like they'd bumped their way over a hurdle.

Laura had wanted Rebecca to talk to Phil, but a rush of nerves overwhelmed her as she looked at him standing on the pier, the wind ruffling his shirt and his hair, so she balled up her napkin and turned to walk away.

Closure would be good, but she could try talking to him tomorrow, when she'd had some time to make sure it was what she wanted.

~

The next morning, she felt braver and more determined, so she woke up fairly early and dug out a fishing pole from the supplies in the lower storage area of her house that she'd noticed the day before. Then she headed out to the pier.

Phil was already there.

She walked past him, and their eyes met when she took a position several feet away from where he stood.

She nodded the way she had the evening before, and he nodded back.

She wondered if she should say something, but she didn't know what to say. So she was silent as she prepared her line.

She'd found plenty of fishing line and a few lures with the rod and reel in the storage area, and last night she'd read a couple of fishing books she'd found on a shelf in the house. It hadn't looked very hard when she was reading about it, and she was glad of the lures because she wasn't too keen on buying worms from Phil's shop to bait a hook.

She did the best she could, hoping Phil wouldn't see her fumbling as she tied the lure to the line with the clinch knot she'd read about. Then she threw the line out as far as she could.

It didn't go very far, but the lure was in the water.

She waited for something to happen.

She waited a long time.

Fishing was a very odd and boring activity. Why the hell was Phil so fond of it?

She looked over at him on and off, and half the time she caught him looking at her too. Whenever their eyes met, both of them would look away quickly.

Her resentment and self-consciousness gradually faded, transformed as he stood on the pier and tried to fish.

It was kind of funny—both of them standing here side by side with their fishing poles, neither saying a word to the other.

She wanted to laugh, even though she still believed Phil had been an ass for the past two days.

She used to have the same experience when she threw temper fits as a child. No matter what had upset her, eventually she would start to see herself as if from outside, recognizing how melodramatic she was being and then starting to find it ironically amusing. The humor would cut through her other emotions like a pair of scissors, leaving them in fragments.

She could feel it happening to her now.

The next time she glanced over and caught Phil's eye, his lips twitched slightly before he looked way.

She had to hide a smile.

He must think it was kind of funny too.

She felt a tug on her line and got excited, so she started to reel it in. But the pull on the line disappeared almost immediately, and she was ridiculously disappointed when she realized that a fish must have taken the lure right off the line.

When she reeled in the empty line, she examined the end and saw that it wasn't broken.

"The knot must have pulled loose," Phil said.

She frowned. "I did a clinch knot like you're supposed to do." Then she added, "I thought I did."

She pulled out another of the lures she'd brought with her and tried to knot that one on, wondering what she was doing wrong.

"Do you want me to check it for you?" Phil asked.

She was about to give him an automatic refusal, but then she raised her eyes to his face. His expression wasn't amused or lofty or pleased or obnoxious. He was asking for real.

Closure.

If she made a few efforts now, maybe she'd feel better for the rest of her life.

"Okay," she agreed. "I don't really know what I'm doing."

"Is it your first time?" He set down his own rod and moved to stand beside her.

"Yeah. I found this stuff at the house."

"You're doing good for your first time." His tone and expression were sober as he checked her line.

He wasn't flirting with her or teasing. That much was clear. It sounded like he meant what he said.

"Is it okay?" she asked as he examined her work.

"I can show you how to make a better knot if you want." His eyes moved from the knot to her face and then back.

"Okay. Thanks."

She paid attention as he demonstrated the knot, and then he watched her do it herself, making a few suggestions as she did. After a few minutes, she felt more confident, and she was pleased with her work as she got ready to cast her line.

"Here," he said, moving an arm around her to adjust the position of her hands. "You'll get it farther doing it this way."

She did as he said, satisfied that she'd improved significantly when her lure went much farther out into the water.

She had to remind herself she was only seeking closure with Phil. Nothing else. So the feel of his warm body behind her, the smell of his clothes and his hair, the strength she recognized in his hands—all of that didn't matter at all.

"Thank you," she said. "That really helped. You're a good teacher."

"Oh. Yeah. Thanks. You're welcome." He lowered his eyes as if she'd embarrassed him. "I do lessons sometimes—with the shop."

"Well, you're good at it." She wasn't really smiling at him. It didn't feel like a smiling conversation.

But it felt a lot better than yesterday morning's conversation had been.

Phil went to get his own rod and moved a bit closer to where she was standing. They both fished in silence until Rebecca finally felt the need to say something.

"I didn't know you lived here." That was what she said.

Phil gave a little jerk. "What?"

"I didn't know you lived here. I really had no idea. I promise I never would have come had I known... I didn't do it on purpose."

"I know."

"Do you? Because the other day you made it sound like—"

"I know how I made it sound. I was surprised, but I could see you were as shocked as me. I know you didn't do it on purpose. It was Laura's doing, I assume."

"Yes. She does that kind of thing all the time—maneuvering people around like they're chess pieces. She does mean well, but it sure gets annoying." Rebecca slanted him a look. "She thought I needed closure."

"What?"

"Closure. That's what she said. I need closure—from the thing with you back then."

"Closure." Phil was shaking his head, a ghost of a smile on his face. "Damn it."

"Why damn it?"

"Your sister and my uncle have been conspiring."

"Why do you say that?"

"Because Russ said almost the exact same thing to me yesterday. I was angry because he was obviously the one who'd told where I was, and he said I needed closure. Those were his exact words."

Rebecca giggled at the dryness of his voice. "I think it was definitely Laura's idea, but I wouldn't be surprised if she told Russ about it. They work together all the time, and they're always coming up with plans. Usually about the business, but still... They might as well be little kids whispering about all their naughty plans."

"I don't think Russ ever acted like a kid, even when he was one."

"He does have that ornery cynic thing going, but I don't know. When he's around Laura..." Rebecca trailed off.

"Anyway, yeah, I guess they've been talking about us needing closure."

Phil had been looking at her, but now he turned back toward the bay. He didn't say anything.

Rebecca didn't either. They fished for a few minutes.

Then Phil finally said, "It's not a bad idea."

"What is?"

"Closure."

"Oh." Her heart was beating like crazy, which was absolutely ridiculous. Closure was supposed to make her more peaceful. Not get her riled up like this. "Yeah. I guess so."

"You want to try it?"

"Maybe." She licked her lips. "I guess it wouldn't hurt anything. I'll only be here two weeks."

"That's probably long enough." He still wasn't meeting her eyes. "For closure, I mean."

"Yeah. Okay. Let's try it."

Rebecca stayed at the pier for another half hour. Then it was getting hot and she was worried about the rising jitters in her chest and belly, so she told Phil goodbye and that she'd come to fish again tomorrow morning.

No use overdoing it. She didn't need to see him a lot. An hour or so fishing every morning was more than enough time for closure without getting her thinking in dangerous directions.

She spent the day hanging out by her pool, reading and napping. She made herself a late lunch of grilled chicken and salad and enjoyed everything about it.

That evening, however, she decided to take a walk again, and she ended up back at the pier.

She hadn't intended to. She was going to wait until tomorrow morning to see Phil again.

But there she was with another ice-cream cone, leaning against the rail and looking at Phil's tight butt.

He noticed her more quickly today and gave her a little wave, so she walked over to where he stood.

She wasn't going to stay long. Just say hello and then continue her walk.

Maybe she'd just finish her ice-cream cone. It was melting like crazy already.

"No fishing gear this evening?" he asked with a little smile. His face and posture were a lot more relaxed now than they'd been for the past two days.

He looked younger. More like himself. She liked to see him this way.

"No. I'm not sure fishing is something I'd want to do more than once a day."

"Too bad. Nothing like it."

"I'm not sure I see the appeal yet. Maybe it will come later."

He gave her a sideways look that was warm and amused and ironic and caused flutters to erupt in her chest. "Maybe so."

"When did you start fishing?" she asked, wanting to distract herself from his attractiveness and because she was genuinely interested. "You never fished as a kid."

"No. I didn't start until I moved here."

"How did you even end up here?"

He shook his head. "I don't really know. I just got in the car and started to drive until I reached the ocean. Then I turned north and stopped when I saw a Help Wanted sign at a hardware store. I got the job and found a place to live and didn't have much to do. So I started to talk to some of the locals here on the pier, and eventually I began to fish."

Fascinated by this abbreviated history, Rebecca could sense a lot of emotion hidden beneath the casual words. Pain and anger and the need to escape had led him here.

But he must have found some sort of peace in the process, and fishing was evidently part of it.

They fell into silence for a minute until Phil said, "Russ told me about your mom. I'm really sorry."

Rebecca swallowed over a familiar ache. "Thank you. It's been six months now, but I still miss her every day."

Phil glanced down at the water. "Yeah. I never knew my mom."

"I know you didn't."

She was feeling too emotional now—and emotions and Phil were not a good combination for her—so she reached out and gave his upper arm a small squeeze as she turned to walk away. "I'll see you tomorrow morning."

"I'll be here."

Closure.

It would be good. A relief. She needed it, and it was time she do something for herself after so many years of pouring herself into other people.

Maybe at the end of these two weeks, she could find closure at last.

Four

The next day, Phil was trying to remind himself that all he could hope for in the next two weeks was closure.

His mind knew this was true.

His body had no clue.

And his heart… wasn't thinking clearly.

He'd woken up excited about the day, which hadn't happened to him in ages. He normally went through life with an easy kind of nonchalance. Not working too hard. Not worrying too much. Not feeling anything that would bother him.

So the jittery anticipation he felt as soon as he opened his eyes worried him.

He shouldn't be feeling this way.

Not about Rebecca.

Not anymore.

He'd been like this about her as a teenager, and the feelings had been brutally ripped out of his heart, leaving nothing but a gaping, aching hole. That was how it had felt back then, and he knew better than to risk it again.

Loving meant trusting. And trusting meant hoping.

And hope was a cruel tease.

That was what his dad had always said, and fate had proven his father right in the most painful of ways.

Phil wasn't a naïve, romantic teenager anymore.

As he showered and dressed, he gave himself a mental lecture about keeping things in perspective. Even if he and Rebecca could overcome their history—which was doubtful—they'd still never be able to maintain a long-term relationship. Not when she lived back home and he was never planning to return again.

Emotional distance. That was what he needed.

He was going to work on that this morning.

Closure and emotional distance.

That was the key to staying safe.

~

An hour after that wise resolution, he was wondering if he'd ever seen anything as beautiful as Rebecca in the morning sun.

Her hair was loose this morning, burnished gold in the sunlight, and her skin was flushed pink from the heat and dewy from the humidity. She was laughing about his description of his business partner, Larry—a middle-aged man who was a brilliant cook but who spent his life complaining—and the amusement glowed on her face.

Her tan shorts and fitted T-shirt also displayed her small, curvy body in a way that wasn't particularly helpful for his state of mind.

Closure.

Emotional distance.

That was the key.

He shouldn't be breathless from nothing more than Rebecca laughing beside him.

"Is something wrong?" she asked, turning her head to look up at him, her blue eyes wide and questioning.

He cleared his throat. "No. No. Why?"

"Because I just asked you a question, and you never answered it."

Shit.

He couldn't even remember what she'd asked him.

What the hell was wrong with him?

"Sorry. I must have zoned out or something. What did you ask?" He was ludicrously pleased that his voice was mostly normal.

"I asked how did you meet Larry."

"Oh. Yeah. I just met him around. You know, when I was hanging out on the pier, fishing. He'd recently opened the restaurant there and wanted to expand in some way but wasn't sure what direction to go in, and I threw out the idea of the shop. He liked it and said he'd only do it if I helped him, so I did."

"Oh. Wow. I bet you never expected that."

"No. Not at all. It just fell in my lap." He exhaled. "Like everything else."

Her smile faded slightly. "What do you mean by that?"

"Nothing. I just meant it happened without me trying to get it."

"Does that happen a lot?"

The question was casual, but there was something knowing in her eyes. As if she still knew him, understood him, saw what his easy demeanor was hiding.

She'd been that way before too.

Whenever he'd had a bad day—when his dad was being an ass, when he'd missed a goal in soccer and lost his team the game—she'd always seen how he was feeling, even when he'd kept a smile on his face.

She used to rub his neck and shoulders for him, telling him he didn't have to smile for her.

He'd never felt as cared for as when he'd been with her.

He wasn't sure why he was remembering all that right now.

She reached out and put a hand on his arm. "Phil?"

He blinked. "Oh. Sorry. Don't know what's wrong with me today. And yeah, I guess it happens some. Things fall in my lap, and it feels like they're meant to be, so I accept them."

"But you like working in the shop, don't you? You didn't just take it because it was the only thing that happened to you, did you?"

"Yes," he said, speaking the truth and not the truth at the exact same time. He'd approached careers the way he approached relationships—never hoping for too much and so never disappointed when it didn't work out or when people let you down. "I like it. It's what I want to be doing."

"Okay. Good. Then it's fine that it just fell in your lap. It would only be a problem if you go around accepting things that happen without trying to change them even if they're not what you want."

She was speaking casually. She obviously wasn't trying to needle at his soul. But he felt the words there anyway. Deeply.

He was thinking about his father, who came from a tough, Appalachian family and was raised to never depend on anyone else since the world would never be kind.

His father hadn't been wrong. His best friend had betrayed him.

Phil had learned from experience—his father's and his own—that the people you love could still turn their backs on you.

It was such a depressing thought he forced it back into a dark corner of his mind where he'd kept it for the past seven years.

Realizing he was losing his struggle for emotional distance far too quickly, he made a point of changing the subject. "So what about you?"

"What about me?"

"Did you start working with your family because it happened to you, or is it really what you want to be doing?"

"Oh." She appeared taken aback by the question. "I guess I never really thought about it before."

"Well, think about it now."

She did. He could see the reflections pass over her face, and he waited expectantly for her to come to conclusions.

Finally she said, "I don't know. I guess it did just happen to me. I mean, my family needed me, particularly after Mom got sick. I needed to be at home so I could help out. But I think it's probably what I want to be doing."

"What else would you do if you could do anything in the world?"

"I don't know."

"Really? You don't know?"

"I've never really thought about it." She looked away from him with a sheepish expression, as if she were embarrassed by the admission.

Her words and her expression made him feel strange. Deep. It was wrong that she'd never let herself seriously think about what she wanted—for her. "Well, think about it now," he murmured.

She swallowed visibly "The truth is, I don't have any grand ambitions in terms of career. I never did. I wouldn't mind being a teacher, but I never felt strongly in that direction. And I guess I always feel kind of guilty about that. Women can do anything now, so why don't I want to do something really impressive?"

"You can be impressive in a way that has nothing to do with career, you know."

"Yeah. I do know that. I still love to cook. I don't want a restaurant or anything like that, but I love cooking."

"You used to want to go to cooking school. Do you still want that?"

"Uh, yeah. I guess I do."

"Then why haven't you?"

She gave a little shrug. "It never seemed worth the time and money since I didn't want to be a career chef. It felt... indulgent."

"What's wrong with indulging yourself occasionally?" His voice was serious, not teasing at all.

"Nothing, I guess. It's just not me." She cleared her throat. "It's not like I'm unhappy. I love being at home and helping out with Holiday Acres. I think I've got a good life."

She seemed to mean it, but it was also clear that she rarely did anything just for herself. And it bothered him. A lot. That she'd poured herself out so much that her sisters had to intervene with this vacation. That she wouldn't let herself go to cooking school, which had been a dream of hers since she was a teenager.

Why wasn't someone focused on taking care of her?

He wondered if she was dating someone.

Probably.

There was no way someone as pretty and sweet as Rebecca would go unattached for long.

It wasn't any of his business though, and he'd probably be better off not knowing.

"So no boyfriend?" he heard himself asking.

Shit.

How had that happened?

She flushed even more. "What?"

Realizing he'd blurted out the question without segue, he tried to cover. "Sorry. I guess that was out of the blue. It made sense in my mind though."

She laughed, dropping her eyes. "No. I don't have a boyfriend."

"Why not?"

"Why not? What the hell kind of question is that? I'm not in control of whether I have a boyfriend or not."

Feeling more comfortable with the shift in tone, he gave her a teasing smile. "Sure you are. Are you saying that no one has asked you out in all these years?"

"Well, yeah. Of course. I had a couple of boyfriends in college. Then I dated a guy for a few months a couple of years ago. And I go out with guys now and then."

"And are the guys always the ones who say no to future dates?"

"No. Sometimes I do."

"So you do have some control over whether or not you have a boyfriend."

She rolled her eyes at him. "Fine. Whatever. It's just that nothing has worked out. And there aren't really that many options of eligible guys back home, unless I want to start tapping the divorced over-forty crowd."

He chuckled at that. "But Charlottesville isn't far away. You'd have a lot more options there. You could find someone to date if you really wanted."

"What's your point?"

"No point. Just an observation."

"All right then. What about you? Are you dating someone?"

"No."

"Why not?"

He met her eyes since her question had been a challenge. "Because there's no one I want to date right now."

"Have you had any serious girlfriends?"

He couldn't believe they'd stumbled into this personal conversation, but they were in it now and there was no way he could go back. "No. Not much of anything since…"

He didn't finish. He didn't need to.

He could see from her expression that she knew the end of his sentence would have been "since you."

Suddenly afraid she would read more into this than she should, he went on, "Not that I've been a monk all this time. I go out sometimes. Nothing serious, but to…"

"Hook up?" Her eyes were laughing again.

"Uh, yeah."

Damn. Why the hell was his heart racing like this?

This morning wasn't going the way it was supposed to.

"Well, I guess that's better than nothing," she said at last.

"I guess."

They fell into silence. They hadn't caught a single fish all morning, and neither of them seemed to care.

Then Rebecca said, "If Larry is such a good cook, maybe I should come by the restaurant sometime."

He straightened up, his heart jumping embarrassingly. "Yeah. You should. You could come to dinner tonight if you wanted. It sometimes fills up, but I could save you a table."

"Really? That would be great. I could come around seven. I love good seafood."

"It'll be good. I guarantee it."

For some reason—for no good reason—it felt like he'd just asked her out on a date.

～

Phil went home at about six that evening and took a shower and changed clothes.

He had three pairs of cargo shorts, and he wore one of the three every single day. There was no reason to put on anything different this evening, but he pulled on a pair of pants instead and paired it with a crew-neck black shirt.

He was still dressed casually. It wasn't like he'd dressed up.

He looked perfectly normal.

He wasn't getting ready for a date.

He went back to the restaurant to grab the best table for Rebecca, the one with the fullest view of the bay.

When he'd put a reserved sign out to keep it from being taken by someone else, he gave a wave to Stella, a friendly woman in her fifties who acted as bartender on weeknights.

"Got a big date planned, I guess," she said with a grin. "With that pretty little blonde you've been making googly eyes at on the pier?"

He jerked to a stop. Googly eyes? "It's not a date."

"Uh-huh."

"It's not. She's just an old friend from my hometown. She's got a vacation rental here for a couple of weeks. It's really not a date."

"Uh-huh. You sure do look nice for a not-date."

Phil glanced down at himself. He was casual. He wasn't dressed up. "It's not a date."

"Keep tryin' to convince yourself of that if you want, honey."

He gave her another wave as he walked back to the kitchen. Stella was just teasing. She was like that. She didn't know the whole situation, and there was no way he could make it clear to her.

It didn't matter.

He knew what he was doing.

He was having a good time, seeking closure. He wasn't getting his hopes up. He was too experienced for that.

Rebecca showed up right at seven, looking pretty and curvy in capris and a V-neck top. She smiled when she saw him, and he showed her to the table.

She took her seat and then looked up at him questioningly as he stood beside the table. "Aren't you eating with me?"

Phil's heart did that jumpy thing again. "Oh. Sure. I wasn't sure if you wanted me to."

"Well," she said with a flash of a smile, "it's better than eating alone."

So he sat down across from her, and they had crab bisque and local trout with scalloped potatoes and salad. Rebecca obviously loved it, if all her moaning over how delicious it was could be any indication.

They talked about the little towns in the area, and he tried to sound informed and amusing. She seemed to enjoy everything about the meal.

Phil definitely did.

He couldn't remember having a better dinner in years.

For a moment, as they were getting up to leave, he seriously wondered if he'd ever had a better meal in his whole life.

She claimed she was too full for dessert yet, so they walked out onto the pier to watch the sunset.

"I do like it here," she said after a while. She was standing very close to him, and Phil had to hold himself back from touching her. "It's different from the ocean beaches."

"Yeah. That's what I like about it. It's... smaller. Purer."

"Purer?" Her eyes were glinting with teasing again.

"Maybe that's the wrong word. I'm not sure what I'm even trying to say."

"I know what you're trying to say. Pure is a good word. It's almost... innocent here."

"Yeah," he breathed. He'd turned his eyes to her face now, and he couldn't look away.

Every cell in his body was reaching for her, yearning for her, pulling him in her direction.

She gazed up at him with her big blue eyes, and he saw her expression transform from amusement to something like awe.

There was no way he could hold back after that.

His hand lifted of its own accord, cupping her face to hold it steady as he leaned down into a kiss.

He brushed his lips against hers, his mind whirling with pleasure and excitement. With a great feat of restraint, he managed to hold back from deepening the kiss, from grabbing her to press her small body against his. He moved his lips against hers, and he felt her intake of a breath, the tightening of her body, the one little hand that came up to fist in his shirt.

She was leaning into him, moving her mouth eagerly, when he realized his body was already responding.

It was too soon.

He wasn't ready for this.

This wasn't what he'd call emotional distance.

So he forced himself to straighten up and drop his hand.

She was flushed and breathless. She'd lowered her lashes but kept darting quick looks up into his face.

"Why... why did you do that?" she asked at last.

"I don't know. I guess I... wanted to."

"Oh." She inhaled and exhaled audibly. "But you still just want closure right?"

"Yeah. Just closure."

That was what he was supposed to want, and so he was going to make himself want it.

"Okay. Good. That's what I want too."

Five

Three days later, Rebecca found herself wide awake at five forty-five in the morning.

She'd set her alarm for six since she wanted to walk on the beach for the sunrise, but she'd somehow woken up on her own before the alarm went off.

She'd gone to bed before ten the night before, and she'd slept soundly all night. She'd also had a two-hour nap the day before, and she'd done nothing but relax for the past four days.

Laura might have been wrong for tricking her into running into Phil, but she wasn't wrong about Rebecca's having been drained and overly tired.

She couldn't remember the last time she felt as good as she did as she put on some clothes and gave her hair a quick brush before pulling it back into a ponytail. She'd take a shower later today—after she got in the pool for a while. For now she wanted to get out to the beach before the sun had fully come up.

It was already slightly light outside as she walked out onto the back patio and then down to the walkway that led over the dunes to the beach.

She was earlier than normal. Phil wouldn't be out on the pier yet. She'd go out to fish with him later in the morning.

She'd done that for the past three days, and then she'd seen him again every evening.

Her time with him felt like part of her vacation. Pleasant. Indulgent. Not part of her regular life.

For the past few days, he hadn't seemed like the person who'd walked out on her seven years ago or the bitter man she'd met those first two days on the pier. He seemed different. Like the sweet, earnest boy she used to know.

But she'd grown up too much to put any hope in their time together. They'd agreed this was closure, and she was holding firm to that knowledge.

She could have fun. Get to know him again. All the while never forgetting that she'd be heading home alone after the two weeks were over.

She never indulged herself in things she wanted to do that didn't have a clear purpose, but this once she was going to do it.

She wanted to spend time with him, and so she would.

It would just be part of her vacation.

She wasn't going to kiss him again though. He'd looked like he might want to again when they said good night every evening, but that one kiss on the pier had been too dangerous, too breathtaking.

Doing it again would be a mistake.

She was thinking through all that as she climbed down the walkway steps and then stepped onto the sand.

Her heart leaped dramatically when she raised her eyes to see that Phil was waiting for her on the beach.

He wore a pair of the cargo shorts he normally wore and a T-shirt with a big fish and a store logo across the front. He was barefoot and holding his shoes.

"What are you doing here?" she asked, smiling as she leaned down to slip off her sandals so she could feel the sand between her toes.

"Waiting for you."

"But why?"

"You'd mentioned you wanted to see the sunrise."

He said it as if it was perfectly natural for him to join her on her sunrise walk.

She was ridiculously glad to see him, and it made her worry a little.

She was doing this. And she thought overall it would be good for her to get closure so her relationship with Phil didn't cast a pall over her entire future.

But she did need to be careful.

She didn't want to go back home with another broken heart.

That would be very stupid.

"Did you want to be alone?" he asked, his smile fading slightly.

"No! No." She smiled as she made her way toward him through the sand. "I'm glad you're here."

His expression relaxed. "Good. Let's go down to where the sand is easier to walk on."

They went down toward the water to the firm, wet sand, and then they turned in the opposite direction of the pier. The beach was quiet, only one runner far ahead of them and a lot of circling birds looking for food.

"How do you stay in such good shape?" she asked after a minute, as she'd been idly admiring his shoulders and leanly built biceps.

"Why wouldn't I be in good shape?"

She chuckled and gave a little shrug. "Well, you hang around and fish all day every day. I guess that's some activity, but it's not really heavy-duty exercise."

His eyes rested on her face with a warm look as he responded, "There's a gym a couple of towns away I use to work out a few times a week. Usually around lunchtime or in the early afternoons."

"Oh." She thought about that for a minute. "On the second day, you said there wasn't a time during the day when you weren't on the pier."

"Ah. Maybe I wasn't being entirely truthful that day." He slanted her a teasing look.

She giggled. "You could have told me to come around lunchtime, and then we never would have seen each other again."

"I know. I could have told you that. I don't even know why I didn't."

"Probably part of you wanted closure, just like I do."

His eyes were on the sparkling water of the bay. "Probably."

There was a resonance in his voice she almost recognized but couldn't quite identify.

It made her feel... fluttery.

They walked for about five minutes before they talked again. Rebecca had been mulling over old memories and spoke one of them aloud. "You remember back in high school, when we played that joke on Scott?"

Phil glanced over at her. "With the cars, you mean?"

"Yeah." She was smiling as she thought back. "He was so upset when he found them all in pieces. And then so mad when he found out it was just a joke."

Phil's brother Scott was a year older than him. He was twenty-seven now and still lived in town and worked as a photographer. He was very good-looking and kind of a player, dating different women all the time. But back in high school he'd been supersmart and just a little geeky. He'd also always treated Phil like a little kid, bossing him around all the time.

Scott had loved putting together models of cars, and he'd prized his collection more than anything.

So Phil and Rebecca had started looking for old models they could take apart, and when they'd had enough, they'd hidden Scott's models and left the pieces in their places instead so Scott would think his models were destroyed.

They'd laughed so hard at his dismay and then his outrage.

Scott had gotten even, but it had been worth it.

"Does Scott still build models?" Rebecca asked.

"I don't think so. Right before he started college he seemed to... I don't know... remake himself. He began to work out, and then he started dating and left all his old stuff behind."

"I see him around pretty often. He does photos of events at Holiday Acres. He doesn't make small talk with me, of course."

"Yeah. That doesn't surprise me."

"I never see Kent at all."

Kent was the oldest of the Matheson brothers. He was a year younger than Laura, so he must be thirty now.

"I don't think anyone sees much of Kent anymore. He's holed up in his cabin, avoiding the world. He calls me occasionally, but I haven't seen him in like four years."

"Have you seen Scott?"

"Yeah. He'll come to visit. Usually about once a year."

She thought about that for a minute, wondering what it would be like to only see her sisters once a year—or once every four years. It sounded terrible to her.

She saw all three of her sisters every single day.

"Our family was never like yours," Phil murmured, evidently reading something on her face.

"Yeah. I know."

"Dad was always… hard. Even before everything happened."

She'd known that too. She well remembered how wounded Phil had been whenever his father got really mean.

It was one of the reasons she'd automatically believed her own father and not Phil's when the conflict broke out.

Another reason had been that it was her dad. Of course she was going to believe him.

But he'd lied.

It still hurt to realize it.

Wanting to do something—anything—to show Phil that she sympathized and understood—she reached out and squeezed his hand.

She'd intended it as a brief gesture, but he tightened his grip so she couldn't pull her hand away when she'd planned.

So she left her hand in his clasp, even when the tension relaxed in him again.

They walked along the beach hand in hand.

It had been a long time since she'd held hands with anyone. It felt more intimate, more special, than it should.

Phil didn't say anything, and he wasn't even looking at her much.

She wondered if it felt special to him too.

They walked about a mile before they turned around and started back. When they reached her walkway, Phil finally let go of her hand.

"I guess you need to go open the shop," she said, suddenly feeling self-conscious as they stood facing each other on the sand.

"Yeah. I should."

"Thanks for coming out to walk with me."

"I wanted to." He dropped his eyes as he spoke but then raised them again to her face.

The sudden warmth of tenderness in his expression stunned her speechless, motionless. She stared at him, her lips parted slightly.

Without saying anything else, he followed through with that look in his eyes. He reached out to brush a gentle hand down a strand of hair that had escaped from her ponytail. Then he leaned forward to press his lips against hers.

He hadn't kissed her since that first time. She'd assumed he was trying to be smart and safe like she was. She certainly hadn't been expected to be kissed at seven o'clock in the morning.

She swayed toward him immediately as his mouth brushed against hers, so softly it stirred nerve endings without any pressure at all. A pulsing began deep inside her—in her head, her heart, and even deeper, lower—as the sensations filled her.

She lifted a hand to hold on to his shirt and opened her mouth without volition, just needing to feel him even more.

Then his tongue was sliding along her lips, glancing against her tongue, and it felt so good she made a little sound at the back of her throat. Had she been able to think clearly, she might have been embarrassed by the little moan, but her mind wasn't working that way at the moment.

The only thing that mattered was the touch of his mouth against hers, the way it was making her feel.

Phil's body was tightening now, and he slid a hand to curve around the back of her skull, holding her steady as he deepened the kiss. Rebecca's body throbbed in pleasure, and she pressed herself against him more fully, needing to feel his heat, his strength.

Before she knew it was happening, she'd wrapped both her arms around him, holding on to his hair with one hand and his neck with the other. Her tongue was tangling with his eagerly, and she whimpered when she felt one of his hands slide down to cup her bottom.

She wasn't sure what caught her attention, but something distracted her. A noise from the beach.

She pulled her mouth away from his, panting as she turned to see a black lab running with clumsy enthusiasm after a ball its owner had thrown.

Rebecca stepped back, hot and flushed and still throbbing with all she'd been feeling.

Phil was flushed too, sweating a little. His body looked very stiff.

Neither one of them said anything immediately.

What the hell could they say?

They were supposed to be having a good time and getting closure, and they'd been devouring each other like they'd been starving for years.

The stupid thing was—the very stupid thing was—she wanted to kiss him again.

She wanted to so much she could barely stop herself.

But she never did what she wanted if it might hurt someone else, and this time the person who might get hurt was her.

With a ragged breath, she managed to say, "Okay. I'm going in now."

"Okay. Good plan."

"Okay."

"Okay."

She darted a look at him again. He clearly wasn't going to move until she did. So she summoned all her determination and managed to climb up the steps to the walkway.

There.

She'd done it.

Now she could go back to the house.

As long as she could manage not to whirl around and throw herself into Phil's arms.

She wasn't that stupid though.

That would be far more than closure.

She wasn't going to do that to herself again.

Six

Two days later was Sunday, and Phil took the day off.

Since he worked almost every day during the summer, he had the freedom to take days off when he wanted to. He usually didn't unless Larry started to pressure him about taking care of himself.

Instead of using his day off in his normal fashion, hanging around watching TV and taking it easy until he went out to a bar in the evening, he asked Rebecca if she wanted to see more of the area.

She did, so he took her around some of the surrounding towns, exploring the beaches and quaint downtown areas with cute antique, craft, food, and primitives shops.

It was all familiar to Phil and not particularly impressive, but Rebecca appeared to love it and find it all fascinating. They had a late lunch at a local restaurant Phil liked that served "home cooking," and they'd gotten bread pudding for dessert, which Rebecca enjoyed with visceral pleasure that got Phil imagining all kinds of things he shouldn't be.

That might have been why he asked out of the blue, "Are you still mad at me?"

She blinked, clearly taken aback by the question as she put down her spoon. "I'm not mad at you. Have I acted like I'm mad about something?"

"I don't mean today. I mean…" He wished he hadn't brought the topic up. It was stupid. Useless. Vaguely mortifying. He was normally a lot more contained than this.

Her blue eyes widened. "You mean about back then?"

He nodded, avoiding her eyes.

"I-I don't know. We're doing this for closure, right? And I think it's helping."

He met her gaze again, an odd, small flare of hope kindling in his heart. "Is it?"

"Yes. I think so. I don't feel so angry when I think back on it now. On you leaving, I mean."

"I did want you to come with me."

Her face twisted briefly. "You wanted me to come with you and never see my family again. Not really a fair choice."

The reasonable part of Phil's mind knew she was right, knew he'd been stupid and immature back then to demand that she leave with him and never look back.

It still hurt, however. Knowing she hadn't loved him enough to choose him over her family.

It had been incontrovertible proof to him that love would always only betray you.

He vividly recalled Christmas Eve when he'd been eight years old and had been waiting excitedly for his father to come home with their presents. He'd been breathless with anticipation. So happy about the holiday. His dad had promised them all kinds of treats.

Then his father had come home drunk instead. No presents. Just a lot of yelling when Kent had complained about their father for spending his extra money on beer instead of Christmas.

The angry arguments had lasted all evening, and Phil had hidden in a closet to get away from them.

That fall from hope and excitement to betrayed disappointment had always been Phil's understanding of love.

That was what love did to you eventually. His father had taught him and his brothers that lesson well.

But Phil wasn't so young and immature anymore. He knew better than to let himself get hopeful and excited since he knew what would follow. He wasn't naïve about love or anything else. And he even understood why Rebecca hadn't been able to let go of what she knew, even though it was her own father who was at fault.

He realized with a shock of pressure in his chest that he wasn't angry with her anymore when he thought back to that day he and Rebecca had broken up.

He understood.

The knowledge changed things. Overwhelmed him.

He had no idea what to do about it.

Rebecca didn't appear to know either. She was breathing raggedly and fiddling with her water glass. Both of them let the topic die.

It was two o'clock when they were walking back to Phil's pickup truck.

The truck had been a hand-me-down from Kent, his oldest brother, who'd gotten it when he first started to drive. Phil had driven it since he'd been sixteen, and he was always having to tinker with it. But it still worked, and he usually just rode his bike around, so it didn't seem worth the money to get something new.

Rebecca had laughed when she saw he still owned it, but she didn't seem to mind.

The mood had relaxed between them again, and she was smiling now as she climbed into the passenger seat.

"What?" he asked at her expression.

"Nothing." She looked almost embarrassed, which made him really want to know what had crossed her mind just then.

"What?"

"Just thinking about this truck."

"Yeah? Me too."

"What are you thinking about the truck?"

"About how old it is," he told her.

"Oh." Her cheeks were slightly flushed. She was absolutely delectable.

He'd put the key in the ignition, but he didn't put the truck into gear. He turned in his seat to face her, a familiar buzzing starting up in his head, in his heart, in his groin. He'd been feeling it a lot lately and was still trying to convince himself it was just physical. "What were you thinking about the truck?"

He wasn't sure she was going to answer. He could see momentary resistance flicker on her face. But then she finally admitted, "I was thinking that the first time you kissed me was in this truck."

The buzzing intensified. "That's what you were thinking?"

"Yeah." She slanted a quick look at him. "Do you remember?"

"Of course I remember."

He'd just turned seventeen and had taken her to the movies. When it was over, they'd gotten into the truck, arguing good-naturedly about one of the plot points. He vividly recalled how pretty she'd been, vibrant and enthusiastic and alive.

She'd always been shy with him before that night, and that evening had been like she was a flower who had finally opened to the sun.

He'd been so bowled over by her that he hadn't had time to even be nervous. He'd just leaned over and kissed her, right in the middle of something she'd been saying.

She'd been surprised—of course she'd been—but she'd also kissed him back.

"That was my first kiss," she said.

He looked at her silently. Then he admitted, "It might as well have been mine too."

He wasn't sure she'd understand what he meant by that, but she did. He saw it on her face.

He knew there was something dangerous about the way he was feeling right now.

It was too real, too intense, too risky.

Too hopeful.

And hoping meant trusting, and trusting meant being disappointed because people always let you down.

She'd let him down when he was nineteen. It had been partly his fault—he knew that now—but the letdown had been real.

But Phil had been living in an emotional desert for a long time, and the past week felt like an oasis to him. Offering him sustenance he needed.

There had been plenty of times in his life when he'd known he probably shouldn't do something, but he'd wanted to do it so much he'd pushed aside the little voice of wisdom. It had always been small things. He shouldn't "borrow" his brother's favorite baseball mitt. He shouldn't spend his entire allowance on candy. He shouldn't put off studying for a major test. He shouldn't hit snooze one more time on his alarm.

This felt the same. He knew he shouldn't let himself feel this way. Closure was all well and good, but he was feeling things right now that were going to bring him real pain when Rebecca walked away from him in another week.

The voice of wisdom kept telling him this, but he didn't want to hear it.

He wanted this. More than wanted it. He *needed* it.

And he wasn't going to not take it when it was right in front of him.

So instead of changing the subject to something less intimate, he leaned forward and kissed her, exactly as he had nine years ago.

She was surprised for just a moment, but then her hands rose to his face. She held him as he moved his mouth against hers, his body tensing around a pleasure that rose so quickly he could barely process it.

The kiss wasn't soft and sweet. It was hungry. Urgent. Matching the deep need that had awakened inside him when she'd appeared a week ago.

She responded to him eagerly, opening her mouth to his tongue and leaning forward to get closer to him.

The old truck had a bench seat, so there was nothing between them. Phil moved out from behind the steering wheel so he could reach her, and then he pulled her into his lap, moving her legs so she was straddling his hips.

She came willingly, her small body and lush curves warm and firm against him. She had one of her hands tangled in his hair, and she was pulling it almost painfully. He didn't care. Everything about her felt good. Everything about her made it clear how much she wanted him.

He was already hard in his pants, and he groaned as she ground herself against him. He couldn't stop kissing her, but he focused enough to slide a hand under her top so he could reach one of her breasts. He fondled her over her bra, thrilled with how quickly her nipple tightened, how she shuddered with pleasure.

She was so hot. So eager. Her hands were all over him, and her hips wouldn't stay still. After a minute, she broke off the kiss, letting her head fall backward as she moaned uninhibitedly.

It was the most erotic thing he'd ever heard in his life.

She was the most erotic thing—with her flushed cheeks and messy hair and the naked pleasure on her face as he caressed her. He brought his other hand up so he could play with both of her breasts over her bra.

She arched back like a bow in his lap and moaned again.

His erection was throbbing painfully. He had no idea how this had happened. They'd just finished lunch. They were getting into the truck.

And it had somehow turned into this.

"Phil," she gasped.

"What, baby?"

"We're... we're in a parking lot."

It was like a truck had slammed into him out of the blue.

Because she was right. They were in a parking lot, and it wasn't empty. A couple was leaving the restaurant right now, walking over toward where they were parked.

And she was in his lap, his hands on her breasts, in the middle of the afternoon.

"Shit," he said, forcing his hands down. It was harder than it should have been to let her go.

"Yeah." She whimpered softly as she climbed off him. "Not exactly what I'd call good timing."

"No. Sorry about that. Got carried away."

"Me too."

They sat for a minute or two until they'd cooled down and caught their breath and Phil's body was under control again.

He wondered what she would say if he suggested he take her home and then take her to bed.

"What do you want to do now?"

"I don't know." She rubbed her face, as if she were trying to make herself think clearly again. "We've got some more time if there's anything else to see around here."

Well, that answered that. She didn't want to jump into bed.

Disappointment.

It always caught up to hope eventually.

As if she'd read his mind, she added, "I know we both got carried away, but I'm not sure it would be smart to…" She shook her head. "If this is just closure, it wouldn't be smart."

Just closure.

It felt like more than that.

But it couldn't be more than that.

If he even let himself think beyond closure, then there was a mountain of pain and unresolved conflict that he'd be forced to face.

It was too much.

Too painful.

Too terrifying.

There was no way sex would be worth it.

"Yeah," he said, his voice hoarse. "You're right. It wouldn't be smart."

She let out a breath and slumped back against the seat. She wasn't meeting his eyes. "I guess we should be smart. Right?"

It was a small comfort to know that she was as disappointed as he was. "Right."

"Okay. So let's do something else then if you don't mind. Is there anything else around here worth seeing?"

He thought. He tried to think. It wasn't easy.

"There's a historic house and garden about fifteen minutes away. It's open to the public on Sunday afternoons. We could go see that if you want."

"That sounds great." She was smiling now. She clearly could recover more quickly than he could. "Let's do that then."

"Okay. Let's do that."

He slid back over behind the steering wheel and took a few more deep breaths until he was satisfied he was in a decent condition to drive.

Then he put the truck into reverse, pulled out of the parking place, and drove away.

Seven

Rebecca was feeling quite unsatisfied.

She knew it was her own fault. She was the one who'd pulled back from Phil when they'd been close to finally consummating the fire that had been smoldering between them for the past week.

Despite her physical discomfort, she still believed it was the right decision.

Yes, she didn't feel good right now. And yes, more than her body wanted something particular to happen with Phil.

But giving in to the temptation would be falling over an edge for her, and she didn't know where she would end up at the end of the fall.

There would probably be a painful crash.

Just like last time.

Indulging herself for a couple of weeks was all well and good, but there were limits to that indulgence.

Nothing in Phil's words or behavior had indicated he wanted more than two weeks.

At first she'd thought he was completely different from the boy she'd known before. He wasn't. He was still just as sweet and funny and thoughtful and surprisingly sensitive.

But the boy he was before had left her. He'd broken her heart.

And expecting a different outcome this time would be incredibly foolish.

She kept telling herself this—over and over again—as they explored a lovely old house and garden and then got in the truck to head back to her vacation rental.

Phil had been good company for most of the day, but he'd fallen quiet now. Occasionally she caught him glancing over toward her, and she had no idea what he was thinking.

He wasn't big on opening up.

He wasn't fake. He'd never been fake. He didn't put on an artificial persona for the world like some people she knew. What he said was usually honest, but it only went so far, so deep. There were parts of his soul he never let anyone see.

If she'd been smarter, she would have realized he'd done the same thing back in high school. He told her the truth—but not all the truth. He'd only ever let her in so far.

It was almost like he hadn't fully trusted her.

And he didn't fully trust her now either.

She was smarter now, and even if there had been the potential for a serious relationship between them, this would have been an issue.

She wanted to be with someone who would let her in for real.

All the way.

"Is something wrong?" Phil asked, pulling to a stop at a traffic light.

His eyes were on her when she looked over, but he almost immediately turned back to the road in front of him.

"No. No, of course not."

"Yeah?"

"Yeah." She sighed, realizing that she could hardly complain about Phil's not opening up when she wasn't willing to do it herself. "I guess maybe I'm just wondering if this is really going to get us closure."

There was a long moment when Phil stared out at the red light and the other car on the opposite side of the intersection. She saw him swallow. "You think we shouldn't hang out anymore?" he asked at last.

"No! I'm not saying that."

"You don't feel better about me now?"

"I do feel better. A lot better. You know I do."

"But you're worried."

"Yeah. A little. I'm…" She shifted awkwardly in her seat, wondering how she'd stumbled into this rather embarrassing confession. "I'm having a good time with you."

He turned back to her at last, his face softening. "I am too."

"So I'm wondering if maybe… maybe I'm going to be kind of bummed when I have to go home."

His amber brown eyes were warm now. Whatever tension he'd been feeling earlier had disappeared. "I'm going to be bummed too."

For some reason his admission made her feel better. Less anxious.

He was in the same situation. He must be feeling some of what she was.

"So what do you think we should do?" he asked when the light turned and he began to accelerate.

"I don't know. I guess we could say goodbye now— when we get back to my place, I mean. That might be smarter." She hated the idea, even though most of her mind was grabbing on to it, saying that it was smart, it was mature, it was the only reasonable thing to do to keep her from another heartbreak. "Things have been good between us this past week, but they haven't gone too far. I mean, too far to... to be hard to walk back from."

She stumbled over the last sentence as she suddenly realized it wasn't true.

It was going to be hard to walk back from even this past week.

But not as hard as it would have been if she'd actually had sex with him.

"Okay," Phil murmured, his voice slightly thick.

She peered at him but couldn't read anything in his expression. She didn't know if he was relieved or disappointed or a little of both like she was.

She made herself relax and closed her eyes for a minute. "It's kind of... kind of disappointing, but maybe it's the smarter thing to do."

"Then we can do it."

When she opened her eyes, he was scanning her face, but he turned away almost immediately.

"Okay," she said, trying to sound confident. "It's settled then."

"It's settled."

She had to change the subject and talk about something else before she started rehashing the whole decision and changing her mind. "Do you mind stopping for a few minutes at a grocery store on the way back? I need a few things, and since my sister left me stranded at the house, I'd have to walk and carry everything back otherwise."

"Sure," he said. "No problem at all."

~

When they got to the grocery store, Rebecca expected Phil to wait in the car while she ran in to grab a few items, but he got out with her.

So instead of a quick stop, they ended up walking through all the aisles, looking at everything that caught their interest and might taste good.

She was loaded up when they reached the cashier, and she was glad she'd had the foresight to bring a lot of the cash Laura had left her so she could pay for it all.

Phil drove her back to the vacation house and helped her carry all her groceries into the kitchen.

As they were unpacking, she caught him looking at the steaks she'd bought. Prime rib eyes. Two in a pack.

"They look good, don't they?" she said.

He glanced up and smiled as he put them in the refrigerator. "Yeah. Are you going to make that sauce you used to make with steaks?"

She chuckled. "The glaze? Yeah. I might. I've got shallots and soy glaze and butter." She paused before she added spontaneously, "I can make them tonight and you could stay, if you wanted."

His eyebrows shot up. "I thought this was it for us."

"It is. I mean, I still think that's for the best. But the day isn't over, and... I don't know... it might be nice to have someone to cook for. It would be a nice way to... to end things."

He hesitated just a moment before he said, "Yeah. It would. Thanks. I'll stay."

Rebecca had the best time she could remember as she leisurely prepared a dinner of steaks, pasta salad, and an iceberg wedge with homemade blue cheese dressing.

Phil helped her do some of the simple things like chop up vegetables and turn the steaks. She opened a bottle of red wine, and they ate out on the covered patio as the sun was starting to set.

At the end of the meal, she was close to melting away from pleasure.

Not only had she enjoyed the meal and the ambience, but she was ridiculously happy that Phil had loved the food so much. He didn't appear to be trying to make her feel good by excessive compliments. His moans and raves seemed utterly genuine.

He'd always loved her cooking.

No one else—other than her family—had ever made her feel as valued as he did.

Between them, they'd finished the bottle of wine, so her mind was buzzing, and she was full enough to be pleasantly satisfied without feeling sick when she finally put down her fork.

The breeze had picked up from the bay and was blowing against her warm cheeks. The air was fresh and salty, and the sunset was casting all kinds of vivid colors onto the water.

She felt so good she was almost embarrassed about it.

She wasn't used to feeling so good, so indulgent.

"That was the best meal I've had in… ages," Phil said, swallowing the last of his wine.

"Thank you. I'm glad you liked it." She smiled at him, hoping she didn't look too much like a sappy fool.

He smiled back, and they just smiled at each other for a little too long.

Realizing how she was feeling, she glanced away and pushed back her chair. "Okay. I better clean up."

"You shouldn't have to clean up since you did all the work to make dinner."

"You did some—"

"I did almost nothing. So I'll clean up. You take it easy."

She started to object, but he was already getting up and picking the dishes up from the table. She watched him as he carried them back inside.

Her eyes weren't very disciplined after all the wine she'd drunk. They lingered on the delicious tight curve of his ass beneath his shorts, and she had the overwhelming urge to go over and squeeze it.

That wouldn't do.

It wouldn't do it all.

She was saying goodbye to him as soon as the dishes were put up.

She didn't want to speed up their farewell, so she didn't try to help him. He would have refused her assistance anyway.

So she got up and went over to the double chaise on the patio near the table, stretching out on it so she could enjoy the evening air and the view.

She listened to the sounds of Phil putting the dishes into the dishwasher and washing up the pots and pans she'd used.

He was a really nice guy.

She liked that he was cleaning up.

Some guys wouldn't have done that.

She liked cooking for him.

She liked that he'd so openly enjoyed it.

She'd liked this whole evening. She couldn't remember the last time she'd been so relaxed.

Laura had been right. She had needed rest.

She had needed closure.

This vacation was a very good idea.

She was so relaxed right now and just a little buzzed from the wine that if she closed her eyes she might just drift off to sleep.

She closed her eyes.

It was so nice out here on the beach.

~

The next thing she was aware of was her hair blowing into her face.

It tickled.

She lifted a hand to brush it back. She hadn't been wearing a ponytail today like usual, so her hair was loose. It felt like it was everywhere.

She opened her eyes as she smoothed it back and realized it was dark outside.

The air was warm and pleasant, and she could hear the sound of the waves on the beach. There was light coming out from inside the house, but the patio lights weren't on.

She'd fallen asleep on the chaise after dinner. She had no idea what time it was.

Phil.

He must have left.

And she'd never gotten to say goodbye.

She turned automatically to look back into the house and blinked when she realized she wasn't alone on the chaise.

Phil. Stretched out beside her. Sound asleep.

She relaxed back, smiling at the fact that he'd stayed. He'd fallen asleep too.

She settled onto her side so she was facing him. His hair was ruffled, and his lashes were ridiculously thick, and his face looked younger than usual. Completely unguarded.

She wondered how long they'd been sleeping.

It was very dark outside. She couldn't see the bay or even the line where the water met the sky. It must have clouded up some since there was no moonlight.

She was actually a bit chilly.

She tried to ignore it for a few minutes but eventually could think of nothing else, so she leaned over to snag a soft throw blanket she'd brought out the other evening. She was settling back down and covering herself up when a thick voice murmured beside her, "You gonna keep that blanket all to yourself?"

She giggled and turned back to see that Phil's eyes were open. He looked soft and groggy. Both sexy and adorable. Without thinking, she spread out the blanket so he could get under it too.

She had to scoot a lot closer to him to make it work, but that wasn't a problem.

"You fell asleep," he said, adjusting to make their positions work. He had to wrap an arm around her, but Rebecca thought that was perfectly natural.

"You fell asleep too!" She nestled up against him. He was warm. Warmer than the blanket.

Now she was warm too.

"I just closed my eyes to keep you company," he said, dry and fond.

"Sure you did."

"Didn't want to walk out and not say goodbye."

She cuddled closer. "I'm glad you didn't."

"Me too." He pressed a kiss against her hair.

Nothing in the world could feel better than she did right now. The rhythmic sound of the waves matched the slow, sensual pulsing inside her. Phil was stroking her hair and back, and her cheek was pressed against his shirt.

"I like this," she said.

"Me too." He kissed her again, this time his mouth pressing with gentle pressure against her temple. Her forehead.

She tilted her head up to give him better access, and his mouth moved down to her cheekbones—one and then the other. Back up to her forehead and down again to her cheeks. Each kiss was like the brush of a feather. "That feels good," she whispered.

"Mm-hmm."

His hand was sliding lower now, down to the curve of her bottom. He stroked her there just as gently as his kisses.

The pulsing of her body intensified, but it was still nothing but pleasant. Delicious.

"That feels really good," she whispered again.

"Mm-hmm." He was still caressing her face with his lips.

"I haven't felt so good in a long time."

"I know you haven't. You need to treat yourself better. Let yourself feel good." His words were a hoarse murmur and as pleasurable as his kisses.

"We were going to be smart," she said, moving her hands up so she could touch his hair.

"Mm-hmm."

"This doesn't feel smart."

"It feels right," he murmured, his mouth lingering on the corner of her mouth.

"Yes." The word came out as almost a hiss as he squeezed the soft flesh between her butt and the back of her thighs.

"Don't you think it feels right?" His body was tense now rather than relaxed, but it was a tension she loved. It spoke of how much he wanted her. She could feel he was growing hard when she rubbed against him.

"Yes," she admitted. "It feels right. Nothing has ever been righter than this. And I really want to feel good again."

He made a little groan in his throat and rolled her over onto her back. Then he kissed her for real.

Both her body and her heart were ready for him, and her mind was falling in line without any real argument. She wrapped both arms around him and spread her legs to make room for him. As they kissed, she bent her knees up so her groin was better aligned with his.

She rocked against the hard bulge in his pants, the stimulation intensifying her pleasure.

He was deep in her mouth now, sliding and thrusting like he was making love to her with his tongue alone. Soon she was nearly writhing beneath him, unable to hold still, desperately trying to feel him more, deeper, harder.

"Fuck," he gasped, finally breaking the kiss and lowering his head to press kisses into the side of her throat. "Oh, baby, you're made of fire. You're blazing right now. It feels like you're going to explode."

"I am." Under normal circumstances, she'd have been embarrassed by the whimper in her voice, but she was far past embarrassment now. "I'm going to explode. Please help me, Phil. I need you to help me. I need to feel good again." She ground her hips against him shamelessly.

"Yes." He moved a hand down to hold on to her bottom. "I'll help you, baby. Let me help you. Let me make it good for you."

"Please. Please. I need...." She had to fight to still her motion, breathing raggedly as he unfastened her shorts and slipped his hand beneath them and under the waistband of her panties. "Please, please, Phil."

Her hands flew up above her head to clutch at the cushion of the chaise as she felt his fingers exploring her intimately.

"Shit," he murmured. "You're so hot and wet."

"Yes." She arched up when he pressed into her clit. "I need to come so bad."

"I know you do."

"It's been so long for me."

"It won't be much longer. You're really close. I can't believe how much you need this." He'd adjusted his hand and now sunk two fingers inside her.

She arched up again. And then again as he gave a thrust with his fingers. Her cheeks were blazing, and her skin was sweating, and her thighs were parted shamelessly, ready for him to do whatever he wanted to do to her. "I do. I need it. Please, make me come with your hand."

"I will. It's not going to take long. You're so ready for me." He voice was hoarse, and his eyes were hot and hungry. So possessive she barely recognized him as the lazy, laid-back man he'd become.

He thrust again. And again.

She gasped loudly and moved her hips with his rhythm.

"That's so good, baby. Ride my hand. Show me how much you want this."

"I do. I do." She tossed her head back and forth and let out an uninhibited moan. "Oh, God, Phil. Please. I'm so close. I need this so much."

"You're going to come so hard. You've been holding back for too long. This is for you. Just for you. Take everything you want."

He fucked her with his fingers more vigorously, and she cried out loudly as the sensations built up to an unbearable peak.

"Don't hold back," he murmured. "Give me all of it."

She came then, so hard she was almost screaming with it. She was never that loud, but something had come over her, something that broke all bounds of the restraints she lived her life with. She shook helplessly as the waves of pleasure overwhelmed her. She clamped down around his hand, soaking his fingers with her arousal. She gripped the cushion above her head like a life line as she rode out the contractions and all the pleasure that came with them.

He kept moving his fingers, sustaining the orgasm longer than she would have thought possible until finally she collapsed in a heap of sated exhaustion onto the chaise.

Then he finally slid out his fingers.

"Oh God," she gasped, still holding on to the cushion with her thighs splayed wide apart. Her shorts were undone, and she was still wearing her bra and top.

She couldn't believe she'd just come as hard as she had.

There was a smile in Phil's voice as he said, "You enjoyed that."

She gave a huff of amusement, unable to even open her eyes yet.

"You needed it."

"I did."

"How long has it been for you?"

"A really long time. Years."

"Then we'll have to make up for lost time." He sounded like he was still smiling when he adjusted again.

She made a little noise when she felt his fingertips against her clit.

He started to massage her there, and her whole body immediately tensed up again.

"Oh God, Phil. I can't. Not again."

"Yes, you can, baby. You can come again and again. I'm going to make you."

"Oh God. Oh please. Oh *please!*"

"Yes, baby. There you go. You're ready to go again already. Look at you. How hot and sexy and eager you are. You want me to touch you so much. You want me to make you feel as good as I can."

She was arching up again as he massaged her clit in slow circles. She was already so sensitized that she'd almost reached orgasm again already. In no time. She rocked and whimpered, "Oh yes. Oh please. Oh please, please, please!"

She came on the last word, and he kept working her over until she came a third time.

He seemed like he might keep going, but she grabbed for his hand and pulled it out from between her legs.

"What is it, baby?" he asked. He was sweating profusely now, and his eyes were like nothing she'd ever seen before.

"I don't want it to just be for me anymore. I want it to be for you too."

He kissed her softly before he said, "You really have no idea, do you? What we just did was for me too."

Eight

Phil was so aroused that his erection was a painful, throbbing presence in his shorts, but he'd also never experienced anything—anything—like making Rebecca come the way he'd just done.

For the past several years, sex for him had been like scratching an itch. He'd needed the relief, and he'd tried to treat the women well, but he'd expected nothing else out of the encounters.

He'd been a teenager—nineteen years old and crazy in love with Rebecca—when sex had last been connected with this kind of emotional intensity for him.

It was startling. Rather intimidating. But also addictive.

He was intoxicated by it. Not just the building anticipation in his body but also the overwhelming pleasure in his heart, his mind.

For a moment, as he kissed her and she pulled him down on top of her, he was afraid he might explode the way Rebecca had done a few minutes ago.

"I want you to fuck me now," she murmured into his ear.

It was the hottest thing. Those words coming out of his sweet, quiet Rebecca.

His erection throbbed dangerously, and his hips gave a few helpless thrusts.

She chuckled and slid her hands down to his ass. "Now, Phil."

"Okay. Okay." It took a minute to pull himself together, but then he straightened up, found the condom he'd brought with him—since he'd been feeling optimistic that morning—and then shucked his clothes as quickly as he could.

Rebecca watched him, her eyes heavy and appreciative as they raked over his naked body. He moved back onto the chaise and started taking off Rebecca's clothes, pulling down her shorts and underwear together as he yanked off her top. Then he reached around to unhook her bra and pulled it off to reveal her firm, rounded breasts.

His erection throbbed even more.

"You're staring." She shifted slightly on the chaise.

"I have good reason to stare. You're so beautiful."

"Thank you." Her words were almost tart, but he figured she was self-conscious and covering for it. She took the condom from him and rolled it on.

Phil was trying not to shake—but not doing a very good job—as he positioned himself between her legs and aligned himself at her entrance.

She bent her knees up around his hips and held on to his butt. "Now, Phil. I want you now."

So he eased his way inside her, both of them moaning softly at the penetration.

She was tight and warm and pliant around him, and nothing in the world had ever felt so good. Sweat dripped down his face and back as he rolled his hips, trying to adjust to the clasp of her body around him.

She was digging her fingernails into his ass, and the pain just heightened his pleasure. He tried to hold still but couldn't. His hips moved of their own accord.

"Yes," she breathed, arching up as he gave a hard, helpless thrust. "Just like that. Please, Phil."

He released a long moan as he let himself go. If she was asking for it, then there was no way he could hold back.

He thrust hard and fast, shaking the chaise, jiggling their bodies. Rebecca moved with him, her knees folded up around his hips. She was making huffs of effort every time he pushed into her, and he was grunting like something primitive. He couldn't help it.

There was nothing in the world right now but Rebecca and how it felt to move with her this way.

"Phil, yes. Please, yes. Harder. Faster."

He bit back a roar as he gave her all he had.

He wasn't going to last long. He could already feel a climax clamping down, and it was going to release any minute.

He wanted Rebecca to come first.

She was almost sobbing, clawing at his ass and tossing her head in her urgency. "Almost... there. Phil, please. Please, hard."

She was tightening all around him now, and she cried out loudly as she fell over the edge. He kept thrusting as she rode out her orgasm in uninhibited eagerness, and then he was coming too.

He roared with it. Couldn't stay quiet. He jerked and shuddered as the waves of pleasure overtook him, and he was still pushing into her hard with each spasm of his release.

He could barely breathe when his body finally started to relax. His lungs hurt. His chest hurt. His throat hurt. His eyes were glazed over. And he could barely hold himself up above her. His arms shook dangerously.

She pulled his weight down on top of her and wrapped herself around him.

They lay like that for a minute, both of them panting and hot and sated.

But there was the condom to deal with. Phil finally had to heave himself up and take care of it. He sat on the edge of the chaise, still trying to catch his breath, and he looked at her.

She smiled up at him.

He swallowed. "So was that... was that goodbye?"

He really didn't know.

She didn't answer immediately, but her expression changed. It flickered with something conflicted, uncertain.

Phil was waiting, almost holding his breath.

"I-I don't know. Do you want it to be?"

He wondered what she wanted him to say.

He had no idea.

So he told her the truth. "No."

Her face and body relaxed. "Me either."

He could finally release his breath. "Okay. Good. Then let's not say goodbye yet."

~

Two days later, Phil went over to Rebecca's vacation house at just after noon.

He usually took a few hours off in the middle of the day since he went in so early and stayed so late, and there was no reason not to spend those hours with Rebecca.

They only had five days left.

He was trying not to think about it.

He was trying not to think of anything except having a good time with Rebecca while he could.

When he got to her house, the door was open, so he knocked on the door and then opened it. "Hey, Rebecca."

"Come on in!" she called.

He found her in the kitchen, setting out dishes on the kitchen bar. She was smiling as if she were having a very good time.

"What's all this?" he asked, coming over peer at what she'd set out.

"This is lunch. I've been making stuff this morning. Chicken salad. Fruit salad. Plus leftover pasta salad. In summary, all kinds of salad except green salad, so hopefully you'll like it."

"Looks great." He was hungry, and he wasted no time in filling up the plate she handed him.

They ate out on the patio, and she asked him about his morning and told him about taking a swim and then walking to the grocery store and having fun with food all morning.

She'd obviously had a good day so far, and her face was glowing with pleasure.

She'd always been like that when she got to cook, and he wondered if she'd had the chance at home lately.

From what she'd said, it sounded like she hadn't.

He finished his plate and then filled up another, and eventually she was giggling at the amount he'd consumed.

He didn't mind. He was full and relaxed and didn't have to go back to work anytime soon.

"Were you going to swim this afternoon?" he asked. "I brought my suit just in case."

She was wearing a bikini beneath her tank top. He could see the straps and was very interested in what it would look like when she took her tank off.

"I don't know. I'm feeling kind of lazy now after eating so much. Maybe I'll get in the hot tub. Did you want to swim?"

"I'll do whatever you do." The hot tub sounded good to him. He was overly full.

So they got into their suits, and as he was stepping into the hot, churning water, Rebecca asked, "Do you want a glass of wine?" She was pouring one for herself from the bottle they'd opened last night.

He hesitated because he wasn't sure how long he'd be able to stay awake if he drank wine on top of the lunch he'd just eaten. He did have to go back to work eventually.

But she was smiling at him, and the wine was white, light, and fruity, so he ended up saying yes.

So they soaked in the hot tub and drank wine and stared out at the waves on the quiet beach. People occasionally walked by, but no one was camped out in front of them or obstructing their view. The hot tub was on the covered part of the patio, so the sun wasn't hot or oppressive, despite the time of day.

And Phil felt perfectly content.

And perfectly cut off from his normal life.

Maybe that was the reason. Or maybe it was the wine. Or maybe it was something else entirely.

But he heard himself saying something he never would have consciously said. "My dad didn't believe in hot tubs."

She was sitting on the ledge seat beside him, but they weren't touching. She'd piled her hair up with a clip so it wouldn't get wet, but a few strands had already slipped free. Her eyes rested on his face as she asked, "What do you mean? I'm assuming he knew they existed."

"Yeah. He didn't believe men should indulge in them."

"What the hell? Why not?"

He gave a little shrug, wondering why he'd even brought it up but not as reluctant to talk about it as he should have been. "He didn't believe men should indulge themselves... in anything. He had those tough Appalachian roots. Work hard. Keep to yourself. Don't indulge. You know what he was like. With us—me, Scott, and Kent—he was even worse."

Phil had never known his mother, who'd died from complications after his birth. He'd been raised by his father alone. Sometimes he wondered if having a mother would have softened his childhood, but it wasn't an answer he'd ever have.

Rebecca's expression had changed now. "How... how much worse?"

"He didn't hit me," he said, reading her mind. "He never hit me. Or any of us. Well, he did hit Kent once, right before Kent left home. They were in a fight, and Kent was in his face. My dad lost his temper and punched him. By that point, Kent was big enough that he could have won a fight with him, but he just walked out instead. But that was the only time... He was just... hard." He took his last swallow of wine and put down his glass.

Rebecca reached over and took his hand, holding it under the water. "He really didn't think men should get into hot tubs?"

"It was indulgent. Weak. And men are supposed to be strong."

"That's ridiculous. Men can get in a hot tub and still be strong. They're allowed to... to feel good sometimes."

"Yeah."

"You feel good right now, don't you?" She let go of his hand and reached up to massage his neck.

He sighed and relaxed back as pleasure spread down from her touch. The hot water was relaxing his body, and he was sated from the food and wine. And there was something freeing about talking to Rebecca this way. "Yes," he admitted hoarsely. "I feel good."

"Good. I want you to feel good. You're allowed." She kept rubbing his neck for a few minutes, and then her hand moved down to his shoulders, his back. "You tell me I'm allowed, and if I'm allowed, then you're allowed too."

Eventually he was moaning softly, shamelessly, and starting to harden in his shorts.

She scooted closer so she could kiss him. He was glazed over with pleasure and relaxation, but he found the coordination to kiss her back. As they kissed, her hand slipped down to his groin and beneath his waistband.

He groaned loudly against her lips as her hand wrapped around his erection.

"I want you to feel good too, Phil," she murmured, giving his lower lip a gentle tug with her teeth.

His hips were rocking into her hand. "Fuck, baby. Oh fuck. I do."

"Good. Then let go for me." She moved her hand to massage his balls for a few moments before she returned to work his shaft.

His whole body tightened like a fist.

"Let go for me," she murmured thickly. "Right now."

He came. So hard and so uninhibitedly it was almost embarrassing. She squeezed him through the spasms as his body shook and he kept making loud, shameless groans.

When he'd finally taken all the pleasure he could, he let out a lingering moan and collapsed back against the side of the hot tub.

She was smiling, as if she were very pleased by his responses. "How do you feel?"

"Good," he managed to gasp. He wanted to reach out and kiss her again, but he didn't have the energy. He could barely speak, barely move. "Better than... anything."

"Good."

It took him a few minutes to recover himself, but then he reached out to pull her closer. He kissed her deeply and moved his hand between her legs as she eagerly responded. He brought her to climax with his fingers, and she came so quickly that she must have been really turned on. She was breathing raggedly and clinging to him as she came down.

"How do you feel?" he asked, stroking her back and bottom under the water.

"I feel so good." She was stretching like a cat against him.

"Good. You're better at taking care of people—taking care of me—than anyone else in the world, but you need to feel good too."

"I do."

They stayed together in the hot tub, wrapped up in each other's arms.

Eventually she said without warning, "You're not like your dad, Phil. You're not... hard."

He didn't answer for a long time. "Maybe. But I think if I'd stayed, I would have become like him. He wasn't born that way either. His father was like that and his grandfather. They were taught the world would always be hard and that people would always betray them. They weren't... wrong."

This was dangerous, treading too close to the core of pain still hidden between them.

But Rebecca left it where it was. Instead, she said, "But you didn't end up that way. You're different. You're not hard that way."

"I hope not. But I'm also not..." He didn't know how to finish the sentence, so he didn't.

She seemed to understand anyway. "You just stay in the shallows, Phil. I can understand why."

He pulled away enough to see her face. "The shallows."

"The shallows. So the water laps over your ankles but you never go too deep. Isn't that what you've been doing?"

"Yes. It's that exactly."

"I can understand that, after everything that happened. It's safe in the shallows."

He liked the analogy. He turned it over in his mind. "You never drown."

"I know." She paused for a long time before she added, "But you also never swim."

He thought about that too.

After a few more minutes, she pulled away from him. "I need to get out before I turn into a prune."

"Yeah. Me too."

They climbed out, dried off, and changed into their clothes.

"When do you need to be back to work this afternoon?"

"By three, I guess. I have to give a lesson at three thirty, and I'll need to get ready for it."

She glanced at a clock. "Okay. Good. Then you have almost two hours to take a nap with me."

"A nap?"

"Yes, a nap. Don't you want to?"

He did. He was physically satisfied in every way, and his body was craving rest. So he let her pull him over onto the double chaise in the shade on the patio, and they stretched out there together.

Phil was asleep in less than five minutes.

Nine

Three days after that, Rebecca slept in until after nine in the morning.

She didn't intend to. She liked to get up early, take a walk on the beach, and end up at the pier where she could fish with Phil for a while.

Fishing was never going to be her favorite activity, but it was mostly just hanging out. And she liked to do that with Phil. As much as she could.

They only had a couple of days left.

But Phil had come over last night the way he had every night that week. They'd lain on the beach until late, listening to the waves and looking at the stars. Then they'd come back to the house and had sex on the chaise on the patio. Then they'd had sex on the couch inside. Then they'd had sex in bed. It had been after two in the morning when she'd finally gone to sleep. Phil had been beside her then, but he was gone when she woke up that morning.

She reached for her phone before she even got out of bed, texting Phil.

You weren't late this morning, were you?

No. I made it just in time.

I just woke up. Sorry I missed fishing.

No worries. I'll come over for lunch.

Sounds good.

She put down her phone and stared up at the ceiling.

Today was Friday.

And she'd be leaving on Sunday.

She was already dreading it.

Before she could start brooding about that too much, her phone rang, and she flipped it open and greeted her sister.

"Hey," Laura said. "How's everything going?"

"It's going good."

"Really?"

"Yes, really. I even slept in this morning. I just woke up."

"Oh wow. That really is progress. I'm glad you've been able to relax."

"I have. It's been nice. I really appreciate you, Olivia, and Penny doing this for me."

Laura brushed aside the thanks, which was her typical response to gratitude. "So are you still hanging out with Phil?"

"Yeah. Sometimes." Rebecca tried to keep her voice casual.

She hadn't told Laura—or anyone—that she'd been having sex with Phil. It wasn't anyone's business, and it would open up a can of worms that was better kept closed.

"Is something going on that I should know about?"

Rebecca rolled her eyes in her empty bedroom. "No. There's nothing you should know about."

"Things are better with him now, aren't they?"

"Yes, they're better."

"And you haven't done anything stupid like fall for him again or something?"

That was like Laura too. All her life, she'd believed that people should be smarter than to be led around by their hearts.

"No. I haven't fallen for him again."

Rebecca hoped—she really, really hoped—that that was true.

She wasn't entirely sure though.

"Are you sure? You sound weird."

"I do not sound weird. I just told you. This was always about closure. I'm coming home on Sunday, and Phil's not about to set foot back home again. He's made that very clear."

Laura was silent on the other end of the line for too long. Then she said, "Shit."

"Shit, what?" Rebecca demanded.

"I didn't make things worse, did I? I never would have done this if I'd thought you'd be stupid enough to fall for him again and then get heartbroken when—"

"I'm not heartbroken! I didn't fall for him. I'm not a child, and I know what I'm doing. I'm having a good time for a couple of weeks, but this is a vacation. It's not real life. I know that."

"Okay."

"I do like Phil, and I remember now why I fell for him before. But he didn't love me enough back then to work through all our issues, and nothing about that has changed. I'm not going to give my heart to a man who doesn't really want it. Not for a second time. I'm really not that stupid, Laura."

Something in her tone must have reassured her sister, because Laura sounded relieved. "Okay. Good. You can think of your time there like an amazing vacation. And maybe Phil will be part of that. But nothing more."

"Nothing more."

Rebecca felt a little glum when she hung up with her sister.

It was clear that Laura never even once considered the possibility of Rebecca and Phil getting together. She'd been honest from the beginning when she said it was just about closure.

Laura was smart. She didn't make up silly daydreams and fairy tales.

She knew what life was like, and she accepted it without flinching.

Rebecca should be more like that too.

Because Phil had never indicated—not once—that he was thinking beyond these two weeks.

She shouldn't even want that.

But a tiny part of her did.

~

Phil did come over for lunch that day. Both of them were feeling lazy, so they just ate sandwiches and watched a movie together on the couch. When he went back to work, she swam for a while and then showered, dressed, and took a nap.

At six thirty, she walked out to the pier.

They ate together at the seafood restaurant. She'd been there several times now, and everyone greeted her like an old friend. She could see from the way Stella, the middle-aged woman behind the bar, was smiling at them that everyone probably thought she and Phil were a done deal.

A real couple.

But no one here knew the whole story.

They went out to the pier afterward. Phil took his fishing rod, but Rebecca didn't feel like bothering. She stood with him at the railing, enjoying the breeze and the sound of the water and the greetings from the locals and a few tourists who passed by.

She did like it here.

She would love to come back for another vacation.

It didn't feel like home though.

She wondered if Phil felt the same way—even after all these years. He always referred to their hometown as home. He never talked about this as home.

There was no reason why he needed to move back, but she couldn't help but wonder what he'd not been able to let go of.

He wasn't likely to tell her. The most he'd opened up in the past two weeks was in the hot tub on Tuesday, when he'd talked about his father. Other than that, he wasn't letting her in.

He probably didn't let anyone in.

And it was just as well since they were saying goodbye in two days.

She needed to just let the idea go, not think about it anymore.

She could be like Laura, accepting the world as it was.

It merely took an act of will. She could do it.

"I can't believe we only have a couple more days," she heard herself saying.

Shit.

She hadn't intended to say that. At all.

Phil glanced over at her, a small, bittersweet smile lifting the corners of his mouth. "I know. I can't believe it's almost over."

Let it go.

Just let it go.

There was no real hope for her here.

"It's too bad we can't... can't stretch it out a little longer." Her cheeks burned, and she hoped the flush wasn't too obvious. She heard the reluctance in her own voice, the little wobble of hope.

Phil might be able to hear it too.

It was torturously long before he answered. "Yeah," he said at last. "But I guess two days can only last so long."

Okay.

That was clear enough.

Two days was all they had.

They'd agreed at the beginning that all they were seeking was closure, and Rebecca needed to hold to that. It wasn't fair to put pressure on him for more, when it clearly wasn't even a possibility to him.

She sighed, blowing out the little glimmer of hope with her breath.

She could be like Laura after all.

She wasn't going to hope for anything else.

~

She stayed at the pier until Phil closed up the shop after sunset, and then they both went back to her vacation house.

They didn't even discuss it anymore. It was understood that they'd spend all their free time together since they had so little time left.

It was dark when they got back, and she opened another bottle of wine, pouring it out for them before they went to stretch out on the chaise on the patio.

They sipped in silence as they lay together.

She wondered what he was thinking.

She wondered if he was anywhere close to as torn about Sunday approaching as she was.

He'd enjoyed his time with her for the past two weeks.

She knew he had.

He'd obviously enjoyed the sex, but it was more than that. He'd enjoyed everything. He was more relaxed than he'd been two weeks ago. Softer. Younger. More real.

"Do you want to have sex?" she asked after a few minutes.

He turned his head to meet her eyes. "Yes. Always."

She gave a soft huff of amusement. "Not every minute of the day."

"Maybe not every minute but a lot of them." He was smiling now, and he put down his wineglass and reached out for her. "I want you a ludicrous number of times a day."

She was smiling as she put down her empty glass and then let him pull her on top of him. She straddled his hips and leaned down to kiss him, already feeling his body tightening beneath her.

She said against his lips, "We might as well take as much as we can before Sunday."

She hadn't intended the words to be heavy, but they changed the mood between them. Something in the air felt tenser. Deeper. More poignant.

Phil claimed her lips again, this time deepening the kiss with his tongue. He stroked her hair, her back, her thighs, her bottom, and he didn't release her mouth.

She was drowning in him after a few minutes, trying to suck in air through her nose. He was touching her all over. Possessive. Entitled. And her body responded with implausible speed.

He only broke the kiss when he pulled off her top. He stared up at her, his hands on her breasts over her bra.

The patio lighting was dim but bright enough for her to see his expression.

It startled her. Made her heart leap in excitement.

He unhooked her bra and pulled the fabric away, fondling her breasts until she was whimpering and arching her back.

They were on the covered part of the patio, but they were in the open air. If someone walked up to the back of the house, they'd be able to see them like this, Rebecca half-naked and astride him, gasping in pleasure from Phil's hands on her breasts.

But there was no one around, and the humid breeze against her bare skin was tantalizing, thrilling.

Rebecca let Phil caress her until she was so wet it was almost uncomfortable. Only then did she start to claw at his shirt.

He didn't take it off for her. Instead, he pulled down her shorts and panties so she was entirely naked. She had to lift her legs to get them off so it was rather awkward, but Phil's eyes were just as hot and hungry as before.

More than that. Something else she couldn't quite recognize.

He'd moved one of his hands down her ass until he was nudging at the cleft between her thighs, teasing her there but never giving her what she really wanted. The other hand was still fondling her tight nipple.

She couldn't stop whimpering as he teased her. There was a damp spot on his shorts now from where she was trying to grind herself against him.

"That's right," he was murmuring. "I love to see you like this. When you finally let that fire inside you out."

"Please, Phil." The throbbing inside her was torture now, but he wasn't letting up. "I'm dying here. I need to come so bad."

"You will. I'm going to make you. It's going to be so good."

"Soon. Please soon." She cried out loudly when he tweaked her nipple hard. Then cried out even louder when he did it again.

"That's so good. So good, baby. Be as loud as you want."

She couldn't help but be loud at the moment, and the small part of her mind that could still process such things really hoped no one was outside and close enough to hear her.

That thought wasn't enough to keep her quiet though. Not when Phil was touching her like this.

He leaned up to take one breast in his mouth, and she sobbed and writhed in response.

If she could get in a slightly different position, she could rub herself against the bulge in his shorts, and it would only take her a few seconds to come.

He wasn't letting her get in position though. He was drawing it out on purpose.

He kept teasing her with the fingers of one hand, giving her arousal little touches but not enough to quench her need.

"Fuck, baby. You want this so much. You're feeling so good right now."

"I am. So good. So good. Oh please, Phil. Please soon." Her fingers were digging into his shoulders so hard it had to have hurt.

She let out a sharp cry when Phil tilted his head down to give her nipple a hard little tug with his teeth. The slight pain caused her whole body to throb dangerously.

"I'm gonna come just from this," she said. "Oh God, Phil, please."

"Okay, baby. You're ready for me now. I want you to ride me tonight."

"Yes, yes. Please. I want to ride you." She started fumbling with the button on his shorts until she'd managed to unfasten them and pull out his hard erection. Together, they put on a condom and he helped position her above him.

Then finally, finally she lowered herself, sheathing him inside her.

It felt so good she started to move over him eagerly, before they could even find a good position.

"Oh fuck, baby," Phil murmured, his face twisting in either effort or pleasure. "Oh fuck, you want this so much. I've never seen you let go like this before. You're wild with it."

She was too far gone to even be embarrassed. She rode him hard and fast, the motion shaking her body so vigorously that her breasts slapped against her chest.

He was holding on to her bottom, his eyes moving from her face to her breasts. "That's right, baby. Just like that. You're so hot. So good. So... everything."

She was sobbing loudly now, riding him as hard as she could. Her thighs burned, and her breasts felt like they were about to explode, and her hair was flying all over her face. But the pressure between her legs wouldn't let her stop or slow.

"Keep going until you come, baby. Don't stop. Don't stop."

Her voice was so loud that it triggered an internal warning, so she tried to bite her lip to stifle it.

"No, baby. No. Don't try to hide it. Be as loud as you want. Show me how much you want this."

She couldn't hold it back. Not after that. She made a series of hoarse, broken screams as her body started to clamp down around his penetration. She came and kept coming as she bounced over him, and Phil was talking her through it, murmuring out thick, encouraging words about how good she was, how much she'd needed it, how much he wanted her to let go.

Her throat ached when the contractions finally started to die. She was choking on ragged breaths.

Then Phil's hand moved to the front of her body and rubbed her swollen clit.

She arched back again with another cry as another orgasm tightened and broke. He kept rubbing her, and her body kept responding, squeezing around his erection in a series of mini-orgasms that wouldn't seem to stop.

Tears were running down her cheeks when her body had finally had its fill. She collapsed on top of him, the shift in position causing his erection to slip out of her very wet entrance.

"That was so good," he was still murmuring. "So good, baby. You needed that so much."

"I did. I did."

"You don't let yourself take what you need very often."

He was right.

He was so right.

One of the reasons this time here had meant so much to her was that she'd been able to indulge in her own pleasure after years of not doing so.

"Give me a minute," she said hoarsely. "And then we'll take care of you too."

"I'm okay. Take your time and recover."

It took a few minutes before her breathing had steadied and the blur of pleasure in her mind had broken enough to allow her to move. But then she raised herself up and straddled him again.

She checked the condom, and it was fine, so she lowered herself over him again.

She was raw and sensitized from her enthusiasm before, but it wasn't uncomfortable.

She smiled down on him. "This time you take what you want."

She waited as he shifted positions slightly. Then he held on to her bottom and started to thrust up into her from below.

He'd been patient so far, but he obviously wanted her a lot. His motion was fast and clumsy, and his rhythm uneven as he rocked beneath her.

She moved with him as best she could, but she let him do most of the work. He grunted every time he thrust up into her, and his body got tighter and tighter.

She tried to talk him through it the way he had, but she didn't think she was very good at it. He didn't seem to mind. He was jerking hard beneath her, his neck arching and his grunts turning into loud sounds of effort as he worked himself up toward release.

When he came, it was just as loud and uninhibited as hers had been. She didn't come with him, so she could watch the twisting pleasure on his face, feel the release of tension in his body.

She loved it.

That he needed her so much.

That he was letting himself take what he needed.

When he'd ridden out all the spasms of his climax, she moved off him and took care of the condom. She went inside and to the bathroom to clean up some and put on a clean tank top and pajama shorts. Then she came back out to the patio.

He was still sprawled out on the chaise with his eyes closed. His shorts were open, and his body completely relaxed.

She scooted beside him, and he exhaled loudly as he wrapped an arm around her.

"Do you want to go to bed?" she asked.

"Not yet."

"You seem pretty worn out, and I am too."

"So let's rest for a little while. But stay out here. I don't want to go to bed yet."

She wondered why. Wondered if he didn't want the day to end yet.

After tonight, they'd only have one left.

Then he murmured, "I don't want Friday to end yet."

Ten

The next day, Phil had to go into work, but he resented even the few hours that meant spending away from Rebecca.

He'd spent the night at her place, and she woke up when he did. But she didn't get up and dressed immediately. Just got coffee and crawled back in bed as he showered and dressed.

He gave her a kiss before he left the vacation house, tasting coffee on her lips.

He wondered what it would be like to go to bed with her every night. Wake up with her every morning.

Impatiently he brushed the poignant thought away. It wasn't going to do any good.

She was leaving tomorrow morning. The lease on the house had run out.

And nothing else had changed.

He went to open up the shop, and he'd set up at the pier and been fishing for about a half hour when Rebecca joined him. She didn't have her fishing rod this morning, but she had a travel mug of coffee like he did and a box of what looked like pastries.

"What's in there?" he asked, immediately interested.

"I stopped at the bakery," she explained. "Donuts."

"Oh. Yum. I'm surprised I haven't gained ten pounds in the past two weeks."

"I'm pretty sure I've gained a few." She flashed him a little smile.

His heart did an absurd little gallop. It really should be used to feeling like this by now, but it wasn't. "You don't hear me complaining. Either about your body or the food." He picked out a chocolate iced donut and bit into it with pleasure. "Thank you."

She nodded as she picked out a chocolate one for herself too.

They ate the donuts without talking, and then Phil picked up his pole again.

"So what do you want to do today?" he asked.

"I don't know. Do you need to work all day again today?"

He shook his head. "Just until noon, when Mary comes in to cover the shop. Then we can do anything you want. What haven't you done that you still want to do before you leave?"

She didn't answer immediately. "I don't know. I can't think of anything. Is there anything I've missed?"

"Not really. We can go around and look at some more towns if you want. Or we can go out to Tangier Island. It's kind of cool. Or we could just hang out if you'd rather."

"Let's just hang out."

"Okay. Sounds good." He tried to sound casual, but he felt heavy, depressed.

He wondered what the hell he was going to do when Rebecca left tomorrow.

He wondered how barren his life was going to feel without her.

It was like he'd been living in his sleep for seven years, and she'd woken him up with her sweet smile and her deep generosity and her hot, hidden passion.

And now he was wide awake, left alone in the dark.

He figured that, despite her attempts at normalcy, she was feeling heavy too. She was quieter than normal, and when she finished her coffee and donut, she put the box and the cup down and leaned against him.

He wrapped one arm around her and held his rod with the other. The fish weren't biting this morning anyway.

"It's going to be a sunny day," Rebecca said eventually.

The weather for both weeks had been really good—hot and humid, of course, but only with a few scattered thunderstorms, none of which had lasted very long. The sun was almost too bright today, as if it were mocking his mood with its unrelenting vibrancy.

When he realized he hadn't answered her, he said, "Yeah. I guess so."

She sighed and leaned even closer to him. "Are you kind of sad too?"

She'd never tried to put on an act the way he sometimes did. She was honest about almost everything.

It was a relief for him to admit, "Yeah. Of course I am."

"I've had a really good time."

"Me too."

Too good a time. He'd realized a couple of nights ago that he'd waded out too far with her, despite his best intentions. He hadn't stayed in the shallows—not the way he should have.

Nothing to do about it now though.

It was going to hurt like hell when she left.

"I guess..." She trailed off.

"You guess what?" His pulse throbbed a few times, as if his body was getting excited. Not aroused. Excited in a different way.

It was a strange and unsettling physical response.

"I guess we couldn't... nothing serious but... but just talk occasionally. After I leave. Or something." She felt stiff beside him, and she'd lowered her eyes.

She was nervous. Self-conscious about what she'd just asked him.

It was a risk.

A risk he never would have taken himself.

His pulse throbbed some more at the idea of talking to her again after she left tomorrow. But the way he was feeling right now was too alarming, too dangerous. He couldn't let it continue—not when he already knew there was no way they could work out everything that had already come between them.

So he said, slightly stilted, "I don't... think so."

He felt something shudder through her small body, but then it was gone. "Okay. I get it. That's probably smart."

"Yeah."

"Closure."

"Closure."

"I guess that's as much as we can hope for."

It was more than Phil had ever known to hope for, but it wasn't all he wanted. It wasn't even close.

~

115

Rebecca stayed at the pier with him until after eleven, but then she went back to the house because she said she wanted to work on lunch.

He would have felt bad that she'd done so much cooking for him these two weeks, but she loved it so much it was obviously not a burden for her.

She said she wanted to make lunch and dinner for him today, and he wasn't about to argue.

He wasn't likely to have anything so good to eat in a really long time. Not even Larry's food tasted as good to him as Rebecca's.

When Mary arrived to take over the shop, he left right away. As he was heading to his bike, his phone rang.

Thinking it was Rebecca, he answered it without checking the screen.

It wasn't Rebecca. It was his Uncle Russ.

"Hey, Phil. How's everything going there?"

"It's fine. Fine." Phil generally liked his uncle, but he wouldn't have answered the phone today if he'd known it was him. He didn't want to talk to Russ. He didn't want to think of anything except Rebecca.

"Anything new going on?" There was a slight edge to Russ's tone, but there was always an edge, so it didn't necessarily mean anything.

"Nope. Nothing new."

"Rebecca's still there, I guess."

"You know she is."

"Coming home tomorrow."

Phil frowned, still standing beside his bike. "Yes."

"You don't sound happy about that."

"If you have something to say, just say it."

"I'm saying what I want to say. You know me. I only ever touch the edges."

It was true. Sometimes it was amusing, but right now it was obnoxious. "Then why are you even asking about it?"

"Because you've sounded different the past couple of times we've talked. Ever since she got there. I was... checking in."

"I don't need you to check in with me."

"Who else do you have?"

No one. He had no one else. He had his brothers, and he loved them, but they hadn't been close for a while, and they never tried to pry into his business.

And he had Rebecca—for the past two weeks anyway.

"Phil," Russ prompted.

"I'm fine."

"You don't sound fine. And if your problem is that Rebecca is leaving, then there's something pretty obvious you can do about it."

"There's nothing I can do."

"You can come home for a visit next month. See if the spark is still there. How hard would that be?"

"I'm not coming home."

"Phil—"

"Don't. I mean it. I'm not coming home."

Russ was silent for a minute, evidently responding to Phil's sharp tone. "Your dad is dead, Phil. Five years dead. Rebecca's dad is dead too. Why not put the thing to rest for good?"

"It's more than that."

"If it's more than that, then tell me what the hell it is. I promise I can find a way around whatever it is. If you love the girl—"

"It's not love." Phil was shaking. He was standing near the shop in the middle of the day, and he was shaking from emotion.

"Whatever you want to call it. If you want to see if there's any future, then you're going to have to resolve the whole mess we've been living with for too long."

"There is no future. Both she and I know it. She's leaving tomorrow, and that's it."

"You're an idiot."

"Maybe."

"No maybe about it." Russ cleared his throat. "All right. You're going to have to do whatever it is you're going to do. Just know if you change your mind, you'll be welcome. I'll be glad to see you. That's not your home up there. This is still your home."

Even that made Phil emotional. He had to take a ragged breath. "Bye, Russ."

"Bye. I hope I didn't make everything worse by telling Laura where you were."

His uncle hung up then, and Phil stood in place, staring down at his phone for a long time. Then he remembered that Rebecca was waiting.

He had less than twenty hours left with her.

He was finally able to move.

He stopped by a shop down the block to buy a bunch of flowers and a bottle of wine for tonight, and then he wasted no more time in heading to her house.

When he gave her the flowers, her cheeks turned pink and she dropped her eyes.

He felt kind of like a fool. A sappy fool. It wasn't really like him.

But there was no way he could feel any other way at the moment.

She'd made a really good steak sandwich out of leftovers from the past two days, and they ate it at the kitchen bar.

They watched another movie in the afternoon, cuddled together on the couch, and then they swam in the afternoon, had sex afterward, then rested until dinner. Rebecca made shrimp and pasta, and it was delicious.

They walked on the beach as the sun was setting, and Phil didn't even mind that Rebecca reached over to take his hand.

He was almost sick thinking about the morning coming, about Rebecca walking away from him for good.

But his conversation with Russ had only clarified it in his mind.

There was nothing else he could do.

He'd feel like shit until she was gone, but then maybe things would go back to normal for him. He'd wade back into the shallows. He'd fall into his old routines.

He'd be safe again.

No hope. No trust. No love.

But also no crushing disappointment when people let you down.

When they got back to the house, they took a shower together and then started kissing as they dried off. Then they were making love, silent and urgent and like they were desperately clinging to something that was slipping out of their grasp.

He pulled the covers up over them afterward, and Rebecca eventually fell asleep at his side.

Phil didn't sleep though.

If this was the last night, he wasn't going to miss any of it.

He stayed awake, holding her all night.

~

He felt sicker than ever the next morning when the alarm on his phone went off at seven.

Laura was arriving at eight to pick Rebecca up. She would have had to get up at the crack of dawn to make it here so early, but knowing Laura, she wouldn't be late.

Phil was planning to be gone when she got here, which meant he had to get up now.

He pulled on his clothes without bothering with a shower, and he helped Rebecca get all her stuff together and empty the refrigerator and the trash.

They'd hardly said anything at all this morning, and Phil's stomach was churning as he came back in from the trash cans on the side of the house.

Rebecca was waiting for him, near her luggage. Her eyes were wide, but there were shadows under her eyes. She looked like she might start crying if pushed even a little.

Phil cleared his throat. "Okay. I better take off."

"Okay." She was still gazing up at him with those big blue eyes, and Phil wasn't sure he could handle it. He reached out to touch her but dropped his hands abruptly.

"I know," she said, her voice breaking slightly. "It's terrible. Let's just say bye and get it over with."

He nodded, swallowing hard. "Goodbye, Rebecca."

"Goodbye." A tear did slip out then, and she quickly swiped it away. "I had... the best time."

"Me too."

"I'm sorry... I'm sorry this is all it can be. *We* can be." It seemed to take courage for her to say that because she couldn't meet his eyes. "But I understand."

He opened his mouth to reply but couldn't get out any words. Instead, he leaned forward and kissed her very softly.

She clenched her hands in his shirt and kissed him back.

When his body started to respond, he forced himself to step back.

"Okay," she said, rubbing her mouth as if she were still feeling him there. "Goodbye, Phil."

"Goodbye."

He turned away from her.

The churning in his gut became a force, an uncontrollable power. One making him stop, turn around, open his mouth again.

He'd never meant to say it, but he heard the words coming out of his mouth anyway. "You could stay here. Longer. If you wanted. You could stay here with me."

Eleven

Rebecca had been steeling herself for goodbye, so she wasn't prepared for Phil's abrupt, stilted declaration.

She stared up at him, trying to make her mind work, trying to figure out if he'd just said what she thought he'd said.

Phil ducked his head, shifting from leg to leg before he met her eyes again. "If you want," he added.

"Stay here?"

He nodded, his hair falling over his forehead. He caught her gaze again, looking self-conscious, earnest, just a little hopeful.

"But... but... I have to give up the house. They only rented it for two weeks."

"I don't mean in this house."

"But... I don't understand."

She didn't. She didn't understand anything, but her heart was starting to burst open, coming alive with a hope she hadn't let herself believe in before.

Phil inhaled deeply and then blew it out. "It was just an idea. If you don't want to... say goodbye yet."

"You want me to stay here?"

"Yes."

"And what?" Her heart was hammering almost painfully, but in a good way.

Maybe this was really happening. What she'd secretly dreamed of ever since Phil had walked out on her seven years ago.

Maybe they could be knit back together.

Maybe the world and all its problems weren't strong enough to tear them apart for good.

His eyebrows lowered, drawing together in a way that made little lines on his forehead. "Stay here and... and see what happens."

See what happens.

See. What. Happens.

All he wanted was to see what happened between them.

He didn't want to make anything happen.

It felt like it had when she was eighteen and had spent all day planning a nice dinner for them one evening since things had been so hard with their families. She'd wanted to try to make things better for Phil, for both of them.

And he'd eaten the food she'd prepared and then abruptly announced that he was leaving town that weekend and never coming back.

She'd been so upset. Crushed. And angrier than she could ever remember being. She'd wanted to fix things, and he'd just run away.

It wasn't like that now, but it felt the same to her. Just as crushing. Just as infuriating. He wanted her to stay here—to give up everything good in her life when he was willing to give up nothing—and just see what happened.

Something rose inside her as she stood there in front of him next to her luggage. Something hot and powerful and years old. The wave of indignation and pain shuddered through her, flushing her cheeks, burning her eyes. "You want me to stay here and do what exactly?"

Phil blinked, clearly surprised by her tone.

When he didn't answer, she went on, "Hang out on the fishing pier with you forever?"

"No. Not forever. For a while. Just to…"

"To see what happens."

"Yes. What's wrong with that?" He could obviously see she was upset but had no idea why, and that just made her angrier.

He had no idea what he was doing right now. He wasn't thinking about her.

"I have family at home. I have work to do. Do you really think that means nothing to me?"

"No. But I thought…" His expression was changing, transforming from confusion to a much harder feeling. Bitterness—like she'd seen on his face when she first saw him on the pier. "It was a suggestion. You seemed not to want to leave. I wasn't saying you had to stay."

"I know you weren't saying I had to stay. But you were acting like it was a reasonable request. Why am I the one who has to make all the sacrifices?"

"Sacri—" His face tightened with anger. "If being with me is a sacrifice, then of course I don't want you to do it."

"Oh stop acting put-upon. You've got to see what you're doing. I know you were hurt. I know it. My family did everything we could think of to make up for what our dad did. We offered you a partnership in our family business, and you threw it back into our face. My dad screwed your family. I know he did. And I know that made it worse for you at home—the way your dad responded, the way he took it out on you and your brothers. But my dad did it. *I* didn't do it. I shouldn't have to give up everything that means something to me for the slightest chance of spending more time with you."

"I'm not asking you to—"

"Yes, you are! Maybe you don't realize you're doing it, but that's exactly what's happening. You won't even consider making a few steps yourself—coming back home and trying to resolve all the painful stuff. You want to stay here in the shallows where there's no chance of getting hurt. Where you'll never have to really open up, never have to really trust someone, never have to feel betrayed again. And all you can offer me is to 'see what happens.' Not even something real."

"Rebecca—"

"No!" She was so angry now she was on fire with it. "No. I'm not a doormat, Phil. Maybe I'm good at taking care of other people, but I've got to take care of myself too. And this isn't doing that. I'm not going to make all the sacrifices. I'm not going to do all the hard stuff, when you're not willing to do anything yourself. It's just like it was before."

"What do you mean it's like before?" he demanded with a scowl. "I wanted you to come with me before, and you said no. I wasn't the one who ended things before."

"Because you wanted me to leave my whole family! Just cut them out of my life. You think that was something I could do? You think that's a reasonable thing to ask anyone as some sort of requirement for a relationship? And then you acted like I didn't love you enough because I didn't want to do it—just move away and never look back. When you were the one who didn't love me. You were only thinking about yourself. You were expecting me to make all the sacrifices. I couldn't do it back then, and I'm not going to do it now. If you can't offer me something real, if you can't love me for real, then I'm not going to take whatever shallow counterfeit you think is safe."

She was hurting him. She could see it in his expression, in his posture. His stumbling suggestion earlier might have been intrinsically selfish, but it had also been sincere.

He wanted her to stay. He wanted to be with her the way they'd been together for the past two weeks.

And she was throwing it back in his face, the way he'd thrown their offer of partnership in Holiday Acres.

She knew how that felt. It was terrible.

But even the stab in her chest at the realization couldn't hold her back. "I'm sorry, Phil. I had a good time with you, and I'm sorry to end it like this. But I'm not going to accept what you're offering me since you're not offering me anything real. You still don't really trust me to work through everything with you. If you can't make a real effort and face the stuff you're been hiding from all this time, then it's never going to be an equal relationship. It's never going to be even a real one. So it can't be anything at all."

He stared at her for several aching seconds, his body shuddering just slightly like he was holding a tidal wave of feeling back.

For a moment she thought he might actually let it go.

She hoped for it. Prayed for it. Felt herself straining toward the possibility.

But he didn't.

He just walked out the front door.

She heard his bike on the gravel. Then the noise was gone.

Phil was gone.

She burst into tears.

~

By the time Laura arrived fifteen minutes later, Rebecca had mostly pulled herself together.

She didn't look good. Her eyes were aching, and she wasn't wearing any makeup to hide the redness of her eyelids or the shadows underneath. But she wasn't crying anymore, and when she greeted Laura, she sounded cheerful. Normal.

"Oh no," Laura said, after scanning Rebecca for about three seconds. "What's the matter?"

"Nothing." Rebecca forced a smile. "It's just kind of early in the morning since I've been sleeping in a lot. I'm all ready."

Laura frowned but didn't pursue the subject, and in a few minutes Rebecca's stuff was in the car and they were on their way home.

They made a quick stop to drop off the key to the house, and Rebecca was relieved that the activity prevented Laura from launching into an interrogation.

Laura's freckles and shiny brown hair were comforting, familiar. So was this car. And the knowledge that she was going home.

She'd been stupid. The world's biggest fool.

But things would be better once she was away from here. When she was back on Holiday Acres.

Where she belonged.

They'd been driving in silence for about ten minutes when Laura turned suddenly to meet her eyes. "I made a mistake, didn't I?"

Rebecca straightened up. "What? What do you mean?"

"With putting you here... where Phil is. I made a mistake. It made things worse for you."

"It didn't make things worse."

"You're really upset. You think I can't see that? I wanted... I wanted you to feel better."

"I know you did. And I do feel better." Before Laura could object, Rebecca hurried on. "I do. I had an amazing time. I got tons of rest, and I was able to really relax, and I had a wonderful time, and I cooked all kinds of good stuff. I loved it. I did. And it was good to... to resolve things with Phil. It really was. I needed to do it."

"Then why have you been crying?"

Rebecca swallowed over the ache in her throat. "Because... well, it didn't end well. But that's not your fault. It's not."

"You wanted things to continue? And he didn't?"

"No. That's not it. He did want things to continue."

"Then what—"

"But it was like before. Exactly like before. He expected me to give up everything. And I won't. I won't. It's just not right. He does really... want to be with me, but he doesn't love me for real. He doesn't love me enough."

A single tear slipped down her cheek as she spoke. She didn't wipe it away for fear Laura would see.

"Shit." Laura was staring ahead, where they were approaching the bay bridge-tunnel. "And you love him. Still. Don't you?"

"Yeah. I guess I do. But I'll be okay."

"I'm really sorry, Becs."

The old nickname made Rebecca shake for just a moment. "I know."

"He's an idiot," Laura muttered in a different tone.

"I know that too."

~

A couple of hours later, they were turning in at the decorative stone archway leading into Holiday Acres.

Rebecca sat up straighter as they took the long drive through the expansive tree farm and approached the main buildings.

The Christmas shop was the size of a soccer field, and it was spilling over with festive decorations and unique crafts. The barn was beside it, complete with sparkling lights strung over the front and never turned off. And on the far side was the big old farmhouse with the offices and coffee shop on the ground floor and their private residence on the upper levels. Maybe to some people it would feel strange to be surrounded by holiday paraphernalia in the beginning of July but not to Rebecca.

It was home.

Before she opened the car door, she heard a dog's ecstatic barking, and when she stepped out, she was almost toppled over by Raven, Penny's seventy-pound springer spaniel.

She greeted the dog, the animal's naked, slobbery affection almost making her cry again.

As soon as Rebecca set the dog back down on all four paws, she was nearly knocked over again by Tommy, who had come from around the building and had launched himself at her.

Tommy was brown-eyed and freckled like his mother, and he was grinning as he pulled away. "You were gone forever!"

"I know. It was a long time. But I missed you, and I'm back now."

"I'm glad. It's no fun around here without you. I've had to hang out with Uncle Russ, and he's always telling me to stop pestering him."

Rebecca's eyes widened. "He is not."

"Yes, he is. He says I'm a pest and so I pester. He says pestering is my natural state, so I can't help but be a pest."

Rebecca glanced over at Laura, who was opening the trunk of her car, but Laura was chuckling and didn't appear a bit concerned about Russ talking that way to her son.

Relieved, Rebecca released the boy and went to help her sister with the luggage.

Maybe Russ had been teasing.

The three of them brought all her stuff into the old farmhouse with Raven panting exuberantly behind them.

Rebecca waved and grinned at Martha, who staffed the coffee shop on weekends, and then she turned to the desk in the large entry hall to see that Russ Matheson was looking for something in a drawer.

He'd worked in the finance department of a big company in Richmond for fifteen years before he'd joined Holiday Acres four years ago. Now he managed the books for the entire business, and according to Laura, he was really good at finding ways to save money.

He glanced up when Tommy sprinted over to where he sat.

"She's finally home!" the boy announced, holding one of Rebecca's small bags with both arms.

"I have eyes, don't I?" Russ's voice was very dry. Much drier than people normally used with children.

Tommy bubbled over with laughter, as if Russ had made a joke. "What are you doing, Uncle Russ?"

"I'm working. Which would have been obvious to anyone who wasn't born a pest." Russ was in his midforties and had the same fit, lean body all the Matheson men had. He had brown hair with a slight sprinkling of gray, a high forehead, and the same amber eyes that Phil had. There wasn't a trace of a smile on his face.

Tommy laughed even more.

Laura was smiling and shaking her head as she came over to ruffle her son's thick hair. "Tommy, no need to waste your energy on ornery old men. Go carry Aunt Rebecca's bag up to her room."

"Yes, Mom," Tommy replied, sounding incredibly put-upon.

"I better make sure he doesn't fall on his face," Laura said, watching her son race up the old stairs. She picked up Rebecca's suitcase and started after him.

Rebecca glanced over and saw Russ had looked up from the file drawer. His eyes were resting on Laura's slim back as she ascended the stairs.

He looked away quickly but not before Rebecca caught his expression.

She'd seen that look in his eyes before.

She wasn't wrong about it.

And Laura clearly had no idea at all.

Rebecca wasn't going to say anything. Laura was so set against romance that it would likely come to nothing, and Rebecca liked Russ too much to put him in that position.

She leaned down to pick up the two shopping bags, which held the remainder of her stuff, but before she could, Russ stopped her with a question.

"You okay?"

She blinked and turned to him in surprise. "Yeah. Why?"

"Just asking." His eyes were always too sharp, too observant, and right now they seemed to see into her mind.

She wondered if he'd talked to Phil. She wondered if he knew what had happened between them.

"I'm fine."

"How's Phil?"

Phil was his nephew. His family. Sometimes it was hard to remember that. The two men were so different, so far apart. "He's okay." She swallowed as a wave of grief washed over. "He's... the same."

"I'm sorry."

He did know. He had to know. There was real sympathy in his voice—so different from his characteristic irony.

Rebecca nodded, dropping her eyes to hide her expression. "Thank you."

She picked up the two shopping bags, straightened up, and then went upstairs to her room.

She was home. She loved it here. She was surrounded by people who cared about her.

It hurt right now, losing Phil again the way she had. It hurt like hell.

But it would get better. Every day it would get better.

And she hadn't made a mistake.

She wasn't going to accept life in the shallows. She wasn't going to love a man who refused to really love her back.

She would be happier without him.

Not right now, but eventually. Hopefully soon.

One day, not long from now, she would be happy again.

Twelve

Phil felt like the bottom had been ripped out of his world.

That was exactly how it felt. Like he'd been safely in a wading pool and a monster had come and bitten out a gaping hole, letting an ocean's worth of water come rushing in from below.

Drowning him.

Five days after he'd parted ways with Rebecca, he went to his gym to work out at lunchtime. He worked himself hard—for more than an hour—so he was drenched with sweat and exhausted when he got on his bike and rode back home.

He didn't mind being tired and sweaty. It was better than having nothing to distract him from the state of his soul.

When he got home, showered, and changed back into the shorts and T-shirt he'd been wearing earlier, he couldn't help but think about what it had been like to go over to Rebecca's vacation house in the middle of the day.

She'd make him lunch. They'd sometimes have sex. They'd get in the pool or the hot tub. Then they'd rest together.

It was worlds away from his life now.

And he couldn't even feel sorry for himself since he knew it was his own fault.

He couldn't resent Rebecca for leaving the way she had. Or even lashing out at him when he'd asked her to stay.

They'd only been together for two weeks, after seven years apart. Of course she wasn't going to move—uproot her whole life—to be close to him.

Who the hell would do that?

He made a sandwich, ate it standing next to his kitchen sink, and stared at Rebecca's blue scarf that was still lying on the top of his dresser.

He needed to throw it away. Get rid of it. Stop staring at it all the time and thinking about her.

Instead of putting it in the garbage, he picked the scarf up after he finished his sandwich and stuck it in his pocket. Then rode back to the shop and pier, feeling glum and heavy and like the rest of the days of his life would follow today in the same bleak monotony.

He parked his bike and went into the office to talk to Larry about some business-related stuff, trying to focus on work when all he wanted to do was sit in a daze and think about Rebecca.

After Larry finished going over everything he needed Phil to do, he scowled and said, "And would you please go get your girl back so you're in a decent mood? You're scaring customers away."

Phil rolled his eyes. "I'm not scaring anyone away." Then he added in a mutter, "And she's not my girl."

"Then that's what you need to fix. Make her your girl, and do it soon. Because all this moping is getting on my nerves."

Phil was tempted to snap a response, but he bit it back.

Larry was always this way, and Phil had never minded before.

It wasn't Larry's fault that Phil was displeased with the entire world at the moment.

He left the office and hoped to make it by the bar without having a conversation with Stella, who was sorting through bottles of liquor on the shelves against the wall.

But no such luck.

"Any word from your girl?" Stella asked with her normal friendly smile.

Phil had to fight not to growl as he stuck his hand in his pocket and fingered the scarf. "She's not my girl."

Stella's face changed.

"Sorry," Phil said quickly, feeling like an asshole. "I'm sorry."

"It's fine, honey. I know you've been having a hard time since she left."

"I'm fine."

"Are you? Because it sure doesn't look like it to me."

Phil had no idea how to answer that. He wanted to end the conversation, but he couldn't bring himself to be rude again to a woman who'd never been anything but good to him. "She... she's got her whole life back home."

Stella's eyes were deeply sympathetic. "And she didn't want to leave it all?"

"I guess not."

"Did you buy her a ring?"

Phil jerked in surprise. "A ring? Of course not. We'd only been together for two weeks."

Stella's brow lowered, and her mouth turned down in a frown. "You wanted her to give up everything she has in her life now and move up here to be with you? And you didn't even give her a ring?"

He stared at the older woman for a moment, his vision blurring as he felt a wave of something hot and strong. "She... she never would have said yes. It was too early."

"I guess. Maybe so. But you at least made it clear you were thinking in that direction? I mean, you didn't expect the poor thing to move here without even a commitment? Surely girls don't do that nowadays, do they? Put up with anything on the off-chance a man might finally step up?"

Phil tried to say something, but no words came out.

Shit.

Is that what he'd done to Rebecca?

Expect her to give up everything without offering her anything in return?

That was what she'd said, and he hadn't understood it until right now.

He'd told her he wanted to see what happened because he was afraid of asking for what he really wanted.

He'd told her he only wanted to "see what happened." When what he'd really wanted was to have her in his life for good.

Without thinking, he pulled Rebecca's scarf out of his pocket and stared down at it. It was pretty and soft and resilient. It looked delicate, but it was strong. Too strong to tear in half.

His breathing turned ragged as he gazed on the blue fabric.

"Phil, hon, you're too good a guy to leave it at that."

"I'm... not a good guy."

"Yeah, you are. You've just forgotten that about yourself. You'll remember. Give it a little time, and you'll remember."

~

Phil felt unsteady on his feet as he finally got out of the restaurant, checked on Mary in the shop, and then got his fishing rod and headed out to the pier.

He didn't have any lessons scheduled for today, so it would probably be a quiet afternoon.

That was good.

He didn't feel like talking, and he needed to think.

Although he was kind of scared to think at the same time.

As he walked down the pier to the end, he passed old Mike Parsons, who came out two or three afternoons a week in the summers. He gave Phil a friendly greeting and said, "Where's your girl?"

Phil froze, holding back the tidal wave of feeling prompted by the question. "She's not my girl," he managed to say.

"Sure she is. Everyone knows it."

It sure seemed like everyone did. He couldn't even go to work without being bombarded with questions about her.

"Well, she's not my girl."

Mike shook his head and tsked his tongue. "All I know is that you've been sleepwalking through life all this time and then she showed up and you finally woke up. To my mind, that means she's your girl."

"Well, she's not. And sleepwalking isn't the worst thing."

"Maybe. Maybe not. I guess it feels pretty easy. You don't have to deal with the hard stuff. But you also don't get any of the good stuff. Not a good trade-off, in my view."

"It doesn't matter. We're not together anymore." It hurt Phil like a physical pain to say the words out loud.

Mike shook his wrinkled head with a smile. "So go get her back. If she's your girl, then go get her back."

Phil managed to return the smile and kept walking to his place on the pier. He prepared his line and then cast it out into the water.

The sun was hot today, and the breeze was strong and humid.

And Mike's final words—along with Larry's complaints and Stella's questions—were all rattling around in his head.

He stood and fished for five minutes, filled with a growing knowledge, realization, understanding.

He saw what he'd done to Rebecca seven years ago.

And he saw what he'd done to her again on Sunday.

When his realization was strong enough, big enough, deep enough, he pulled his line back in.

Then he got his stuff together, returned to the shop, stopped by the office to have a brief conversation with Larry, and he headed back to his apartment.

Fifteen minutes later, he was filling his old pickup truck with gas and pulling out onto the road.

Mike was right.

He'd been sleepwalking through life. Trying to escape all the hard stuff. Waiting for people to let him down the way his father always said they would.

So maybe he'd managed to avoid some of the hard things, but he'd also never got any of the good.

He wasn't going to do it anymore.

Rebecca was his girl. Everyone knew it.

He'd known it since he was seventeen years old and had been so awed by the fire inside her he'd had to kiss her in the front seat of this truck.

He was going to get her back.

~

A few hours later, he was pulling into the long driveway in front of Russ's hundred-year-old farmhouse.

He hadn't called anyone to tell them he was coming, but he could see Russ's car parked under the carport, so he was obviously home.

It was getting dark. Part of him wanted to head right to Holiday Acres and find Rebecca, but as he'd gotten closer to town, he'd also started feeling heavier, more anxious.

It wasn't as simple as pulling Rebecca into his arms.

He knew it, and he'd known it when he got into his truck to come here.

There was more that he'd have to do here.

He went to the front door and knocked, waiting a minute before he heard the dead bolt turn and the door start to open.

Russ blinked at him through the storm door.

Phil just stood there. He had no idea what to say.

Finally Russ opened the storm door, but he didn't step out of the way. "Why are you here?" he asked.

It wasn't a very welcoming greeting, but it also didn't sound rude. It sounded... bewildered.

"I... You were right."

"I know I was right. But how right do you think I was? Because I'm happy to see you, Phil, but I'm not okay

140

with you coming here and blowing the ground out from under good people's lives and leaving a mess behind you. So how right do you think I was?"

Phil felt an automatic tensing of defensiveness, but he let it go immediately.

He deserved the question. He knew he did.

"I don't want to blow things apart. You were right about everything."

"If you're not ready for all of it, then you're going to hurt her even more."

"She's hurt?" The question was embarrassingly hopeful. He didn't want Rebecca to suffer, but he hoped she was missing him at least a little.

"Of course she's hurt. You broke her heart. Again." Russ didn't look angry even now. He looked wary.

"I broke my heart too. I've been doing it for years. I want everything. I... think I'm ready."

Russ scanned his face with his unnervingly astute eyes. Then his expression finally relaxed into a smile. "About time. Come on in."

~

The next morning, as Phil was drinking coffee on his uncle's front porch, a car turned into the driveway and parked behind his truck.

He didn't recognize the vehicle. It was an expensive dark gray SUV, and he couldn't see the driver through the darkened windows.

He was surprised that Russ would have a visitor at six in the morning, but Phil didn't know much about his uncle anymore.

When a man got out of the driver's side, Phil understood what he was doing here.

It was his brother, Scott, who was a year older than him.

Scott was taller and darker than him, but their features and eyes were the same. Scott wasn't smiling as he came up and sat on the rocking chair next to Phil.

"Did Russ call you?" Phil asked.

"Yes. At ten o'clock last night. You could have called before you showed up, you know."

"I know."

They sat there in silence for a while.

"You're doing okay?" Phil asked at last when the quiet started to become awkward.

"Yeah. Work's good. Everything else is fine." Scott turned to peer at Phil closely. "So you're going to get together with Rebecca?"

"I don't know. I don't even know if she'll have me."

"But you're going to try?"

"Yes. I'm going to try." He paused, feeling weird and deep and uncomfortable. He wasn't used to this. He hadn't felt this way for years. "What happened wasn't her fault."

"I know."

The words surprised Phil since Scott had always been as bitter as he'd been himself.

"You know?"

Scott sighed. He was the smartest of the three brothers, but he'd always known how to laugh. Sometime in college he'd turned into a player. He wasn't usually serious like this—any more than Phil was. "Yes. I know. To tell you the truth, I'm kind of tired of the whole wretched mess. Look what it did to Dad and Holiday."

Phil flinched slightly. "The fight wasn't what killed them."

The two men had been killed in a fluke, a random accident. They'd been at a town council meeting—arguing like normal at the front of the room—and a trucker who'd been driving through town had fallen asleep and plowed right into the building, killing both men instantly.

It had been horrible. Shocking. But they hadn't been killed because they were fighting. It couldn't be explained away that way.

"I know," Scott said, sounding more tired than ever. "But they took the fucking fight to their graves, and I'm not sure I want to do that. If you want to get over it, I'm not going to blame you."

Phil relaxed slightly, relieved that at least one of his brothers wasn't going to resent his attempt at reconciliation. "Have you talked to any of the Holidays lately? Weren't you in the same class as Olivia?"

"Yeah. Olivia doesn't like me. At all. She's not like Rebecca. She doesn't want to be my friend." Scott sounded almost amused, so obviously he wasn't unduly concerned by this state of affairs. "But Rebecca was always into you. I bet she still is."

Phil wasn't as convinced as his brother, but he had hope for the first time. He said as he finished his coffee, "I sure hope so."

Thirteen

Rebecca slept in until almost eight, and she didn't even feel guilty about it.

She'd stayed up late the evening before, baking cupcakes to sell in the coffee shop. She'd had a good time, and they'd come out really well. So she was proud of the cupcakes and hoped they'd sell on the pastry trays in the shop. But she was tired when she woke up at seven, so she stayed in bed an extra hour.

She showered and dressed in capris and a casual top, and then she went downstairs to see what was going on.

Laura was working in the office, and Tommy was "helping" Chuck and Ed inspect some trees. Olivia was in town playing nice to a local vendor. Penny was at a craft show in Asheville. And evidently Russ was coming in late today.

Since everything was quiet, Rebecca had to look around for something to do. When she saw that several boxes had arrived yesterday and hadn't yet been unpacked, she opened them, delighted when she discovered that they were filled with handmade ornaments by a pair of her favorite craftspeople.

The Mikhelsons lived in a mountain county in southwest Virginia, and Holiday Acres had been stocking their ornaments for more than ten years now. Rebecca gushed over every piece she pulled out of the boxes. Beautifully carved and painted figures of men and women with quaint hand-sewn clothes and accessories.

Last year, they'd sold out of the Mikhelsons' ornaments in October, so they'd ordered twice as many this year.

Olivia came into the storeroom while Rebecca was opening the last box.

"Oh!" Olivia said. "The Mikhelsons' stuff came?"

"Yes. You should see them this year. They're exquisite."

Olivia was probably the prettiest of the four Holiday sisters, and she certainly put the most effort into her appearance. Her hair was golden brown and shiny and perfectly cut to swing around her shoulders. Her eyes were blue, her skin was fresh and clear, and her makeup always perfectly done. Today she wore a pair of stylish trousers and a sleeveless top that showed off her long slim arms and neck. She also wore designer heels and pretty gold jewelry.

Rebecca occasionally felt not quite dressed in the presence of her sister, but she didn't let it worry her the way she had when she was younger.

"Look at these," she said, holding up a lovely bride-and-groom set of ornaments, complete with boutonniere in the groom's lapel.

"I love them!"

They oohed and aahed over the ornaments for a few minutes until the final box was unpacked.

Then Olivia asked, "So how are you doing today?"

"I'm fine."

"Really?"

"Yes. And honestly I'm a little tired of everyone asking me that."

"Well, we're worried about you. You can't blame us. We thought the vacation would be good for you."

"It was good for me."

"But you came home with a broken heart."

Rebecca swallowed over a lump in her throat and managed to smile. "It's not the end of the world."

"I could just strangle Phil. I really could."

"Don't be that way."

"I will be that way. Every one of the Matheson boys is an asshole. It's amazing the family couldn't turn up with one decent man."

"Russ is decent."

Olivia nodded, her shiny hair swinging over her shoulders. "Well, yeah. Russ is okay—or he would be if he wasn't always sarcastic. But the sons..." She shook her head. "I see Scott out with a different woman every weekend. Talk about an asshole."

"There's nothing wrong with dating a lot, as long as you're honest with the—"

"You really think all those girls want to just be the flavor of the week for him?"

"No. I'm sure they're hoping they'll be the one to tame him at last." Rebecca sighed. "But Phil was never really like that. He was always..."

"An asshole."

"He's not an asshole. Not really."

"You're seriously defending him to me? After what he did to you?"

"He didn't do anything that bad. He just wouldn't commit. He's still into me. I know he is. But not enough to get over all the mess from the past and trust me enough to make a real commitment. He didn't do it on purpose to hurt me."

"But he hurt you anyway, and I'm not okay with that." Olivia made an exaggerated pouting face, which made Rebecca giggle. "I guess he's probably a little better than Scott. But not much."

"It doesn't matter anyway. I'm not likely to ever see him again."

Olivia reached over and put a hand over Rebecca's, and the silent gesture made Rebecca's eyes burn.

Then she straightened her shoulders and gave her sister a wobbly smile. "I'm fine. I really am. I'm going to be fine."

"I know you will be. And you definitely don't want a guy who'd expect you to make all the sacrifices when he wasn't willing to make any himself. You would have had to move!"

"I'd have been willing to move. Really, I would. It wasn't because I have to stay here for the rest of my life. That's not what it was about."

"I know. You need it to be equal."

"Exactly." Rebecca blew out a breath and forced herself not to dwell on might-have-beens. "Anyway, I might be moving after all. For a short time."

"Really? Why?"

"I applied to that cooking school in Richmond. I did it after all."

Olivia squealed in excitement and leaned over to hug Rebecca, and both of them were grinning as they pulled apart. "I'm so proud of you. You've wanted to do it forever and never would."

"I didn't think there would be enough of a payoff for the time and effort. But I've been thinking a lot, and I do have a habit of denying myself things I really want to do. I can take care of other people and still take care of myself. So I'm going to try to get more of a balance on that. I want to do this cooking school, so I will."

"You definitely should. You'll have so much fun. And I can't wait for you to cook something for me when you come back."

Rebecca was genuinely excited about the possibility. It gave her something to look forward to, other than day after day without Phil.

It still ached. Still felt brutally wrong that he hadn't even given them a chance.

But her life was still important, and she was going to keep working on it—with or without him.

She hoped he was okay.

She was about to reply to Olivia when her phone chimed with text.

It was Laura. *Need you out here.*

Rebecca frowned and showed the text to Olivia.

"That's weird," Olivia said, standing up and brushing off her trousers.

"I know. I better see what she wants."

Olivia came with her as she left the storeroom and walked down the hall to the offices. Rebecca pulled to an abrupt stop when she stepped into the reception area and saw who was leaning against the wall in the entryway.

Phil.

Wearing a fish T-shirt and his cargo shorts. Lean and tanned and tired-looking.

He straightened up as she arrived, and his eyes scanned her face urgently, almost hungrily.

Rebecca was frozen. Her mind couldn't process it. She just stared, her lips parted slightly.

Laura was standing near the desk with her arms crossed over her chest. She didn't look at all welcoming, and she didn't sound it either as she said, "I'll send him away if you want."

Rebecca turned back to Phil, and a pressure in her chest threatened to suffocate her. She still couldn't say anything.

"Rebecca?" Laura prompted. "If he's just going to make things worse, it'll be better if I send him away."

"I'm not going to make things worse." Phil sounded earnest, sincere, rather than defensive. "I want to make things better if I can."

Rebecca's hands were shaking, so she tightened them into fists at her side.

"Can we talk?" Phil asked more softly, holding her gaze.

She gave a jerky nod. Then she turned to Laura, who was looking at her questioningly. She nodded again, and Laura relaxed just slightly. "Olivia and I will be right here. Come find us if you need us."

Olivia gave Rebecca's arm a quick squeeze as she walked by, her expression a lot more excited than Laura's.

Rebecca stood where she was until Phil stepped over to her. "Is there somewhere we can talk?" he asked.

She nodded again since that was the only way she seemed to be able to communicate at the moment. Then she gestured up the stairs.

She and Phil walked up to a cozy sitting room in their private residence upstairs, complete with a fireplace and huge windows looking down onto the field of trees.

Rebecca lowered herself to perch on the edge of a wingback chair and folded her trembling hands on her lap. "What are you doing here?" she asked, amazed that her voice was still capable of working.

"I wanted to see you." He sat down on the chair next to her, leaning forward.

"But why?"

"Because…" His voice caught in his throat, and he glanced away. Then met her eyes again as he said, "Because I was wrong."

"You were wrong?"

"I was wrong. Selfish. Expecting too much from you when I wasn't willing to give you anything. I was wrong. And I'm really sorry, Rebecca."

Now she was shaking all over. It was rather embarrassing. "You are?"

His eyes were very soft, very sober. "I am. And whatever I need to do to have a chance with you again, I'll do."

A squeaky sound came out of her throat.

"I know I don't deserve a second chance with you," Phil went on, his voice still hoarse but also urgent, passionate. "It's twice now I walked away from what I could have had with you, and that's two times too many. But I'm not going to do it again. So I'm wondering if there's any way I could… I could have one more try."

"I-I don't know." She wrapped her arms across her belly to try to stop herself from shaking, but it didn't work. It felt like her head, her chest, her soul was about to explode with feeling, but there were too many feelings at once.

They were scaring her.

She wasn't sure she was able to handle them.

"I know I don't deserve it."

"It's not—it's not that. It's that I was... I've been trying to start my life again, trying to be better... for myself. And I don't know if I can go back."

"We don't have to go back. We can go forward."

"Can we?"

"I-I hope so." His mouth twisted just briefly. "You don't want to go forward with me anymore?"

"I do. But... I'm scared. Worried."

"That's okay."

"I don't want to just jump into something again and then have the same thing happen again. I-I can't do that to myself. Not again."

"I know you can't. You shouldn't. I can wait. We can go slow. We can just talk. Maybe. Nothing more. Until you feel more comfortable." He was trying very hard to sound calm and gentle, but she could see deep feeling barely contained in his eyes. Like the slightest push would unleash it.

It was terrifying and thrilling at once.

She sucked in a ragged breath and clung to the safety net he'd offered. She needed it. She needed something. It felt like the top of her head would explode with all the emotions churning through her. "That would be okay with you? If we just... talk. For a while. If we go really slow?"

"Of course it would be okay." He had to clear his throat since it was breaking on each word. He leaned forward and took both her hands in his, holding them tightly. "Rebecca, so you think that would be okay? If we just talk, keep in touch? See if you can... trust me again?"

She managed to nod, her face contorting as she tried to control her emotions. "I'd like to. Nothing... definite. But I'd like to try."

He made a choked sound and lowered his head, his whole upper body. For just a moment his forehead was touching their clasped hands. She thought he muttered, "Oh thank God" before he straightened up again.

When he did, he was smiling. "We can go as slow as you want. I know you have no reason to trust that I'm ready to commit. But I am. I want to let go of all the anger and bitterness of the past. I want to move forward. I want to... I want to get out of the shallows. I want to swim. I think I'm ready."

A tear slipped out of one eye, but she was smiling at him too. "I'm so glad, Phil. No matter what else happens, I'm so glad."

He was breathing heavily, his eyes devouring her face. "Is it all right if I hug you?"

She nodded at him stupidly.

He reached out and pulled her against him, slightly awkward since they were both sitting on the edges of different chairs, but Rebecca had no complaints. His body was warm and strong and familiar, and his arms held her close.

"I can't believe you finally came home," she said as they finally pulled apart.

"I know. I can't believe it myself. But the funny thing is it wasn't as traumatic as I always assumed it would be. It's been... kind of nice. It's smaller than I remember. Not as... bleak."

"So you think you could come visit again?"

His eyes were still smiling even though his mouth was sober again. "Of course I will. If you want me to, I'll come as often as I can."

"And I can come visit you too. Sometimes."

"Really?"

"Yes. Really. I like it there. It will be nice. And we can... go slow."

"As slow as you want. I won't even kiss you until you're ready."

"I think that's probably best. I'm not trying to make you suffer or anything, but I'm not... I'm not totally sure of this yet. I don't want to... jump into the deep end until I'm sure... It's just that I've spent so long doing things for other people without doing what's best for me. And so I want—"

"Rebecca," Phil broke in, reaching out for one of her hands. "You don't have to explain it to me. I understand. And I'm not disappointed. At all."

"You're not?"

"Look at me."

She did. She looked at him closely, taking in his flushed cheeks and his tense posture and the way his mouth kept twitching up at the corners and the blaze of excitement, of joy, of awe in his eyes.

He wasn't disappointed.

He was thrilled.

And so she could be thrilled too.

"Okay," she said, lowering her lashes as her skin warmed with pleasure. Then she raised her eyes and said in a different tone, "I applied for cooking school."

"Really?"

"Yeah. The one in Richmond. If I get in, I'm going to do it."

He reached out to hug her again, and she felt so proud as well as happy.

Like sharing it with him was as good as doing it in the first place.

She knew for sure she'd done the right thing.

~

Phil stayed for lunch—which wasn't as bad as it could have been, considering they ate with Laura, Olivia, Russ, and Tommy. Rebecca knew her sisters were less likely to trust Phil than she was, but no one argued and everyone made an effort to be congenial.

Overall, it was good, and then Rebecca showed Phil all around Holiday Acres, and then they went to visit their fathers' graves—in different corners of the same cemetery.

He talked about his father a little. Not a lot but it was a start.

He was trying.

It meant something to her.

She wanted to jump in with him all the way, but it still felt too ephemeral. She needed confirmation that this was real, that it was forever, and she hadn't gotten it yet.

Phil had taken the day off from work, but he did need to get back before tomorrow since Saturdays were his busiest day. So they said goodbye at about three in the afternoon before she left to take Tommy into town to buy some new shoes.

She was happy and excited when she returned home with Tommy an hour later. Phil was gone, of course, but he'd promised to call that evening.

They could talk a lot. They could see each other a couple of times a month since the three-hour drive between them wasn't really very long.

They could go slow.

Rebecca suspected it wouldn't take her very long to know for sure that Phil was ready to commit, but she wasn't going to go all in until she was positive.

She wasn't going to do that to herself again.

When she parked her car, Tommy ran off to watch Ed on a tractor, leaving Rebecca to take his shoes inside.

She found Olivia and Laura in the office, and she frowned at their expressions. "What's wrong?"

"Come sit down," Laura said.

Rebecca set down the bag and walked over, a knot of fear tightening in her gut. "What's wrong? What happened?"

Olivia met Laura's eyes with an expression that made Rebecca's heart lurch.

"Tell me," she demanded. "What's going on? You're scaring me."

"It's nothing bad," Laura said. "At least I don't think it's bad. It's just surprising. At least it surprised me."

"What did? Tell me what's going on right now."

"Are you really okay with how things are with Phil?" Olivia asked.

"Yes. Yes, of course I am. I'm happy about it. I'm afraid to let myself be any happier since I'm still not sure... I just need to be really sure that he's serious about committing, about putting the past to rest. But I think he is. We're going to go slow, but you know he's always been the one for me."

"I know. Everyone always knew it. You've been a couple for most of your life, even when you were apart." Olivia was smiling now.

Laura rolled her eyes. "Don't be silly. See, here's the thing, Becs. Phil talked to Russ and me after you left with Tommy."

Rebecca froze. "What?"

"He talked to us. About that partnership deal we offered him four years ago. He wanted to sign it."

"*What?*" This time the word was barely a rasp.

"I guess he's pretty serious about the whole thing. I'm naturally suspicious, but I don't know how we can doubt this." She handed Rebecca a stack of papers. "We worked it all out exactly as he wanted. He's accepted the share we offered him, but he doesn't want to be involved the way Russ is. And he doesn't want to take the profits. He wants to roll his share of the profits back into a fund we can use for community outreach, giving local girls and boys a chance to develop their gifts. That's what he said, so that's what we wrote up. He's signed it. It's a done deal. I think... I think he's as serious as serious can get."

"He's crazy in love with you, Rebecca," Olivia said. "It's written all over his face. I think he's really trying to put the past to rest so he's free to love you the way he needs to."

Rebecca's vision had blurred over, and she couldn't catch her breath. She was staring down at the top page of the contract in her hands.

This was it. A symbol. Confirmation.

She knew now that Phil was ready. That this was real.

"Rebecca," Laura prompted when she couldn't get anything said. "Is this okay? I thought you'd be happy about it. Even I can't deny that the man has got it bad for you and he's really trying to turn his life around."

Rebecca made an embarrassing sobbing sound.

Olivia laughed. "I think that means it's okay with her."

"I'm sure!" Rebecca burst out, her voice suddenly freed. "I'm sure now. I'm sure about him!"

Olivia clapped her hands with a little squeal.

Laura shook her head. "That didn't take long, did it?"

"I'm sure," Rebecca said again. "I'm sure now."

"So maybe give him a call," Laura suggested.

"No, no," Olivia said. "Calling isn't enough. You should go see him."

"But he just came here."

"So? Why should that stop you?"

"You mean drive out to the Eastern Shore again?"

"Yes. Why not?"

"Because he was just here."

"So? What's your point? Do you want to see him or not?" Olivia demanded.

"Of course I want to see him."

"So get in your car and go. You'll just be an hour or so behind him. I guarantee he's going to want to see you in person when you tell him you're sure."

Rebecca glanced over at Laura, who just shrugged. "Tommy's not going to be happy when he finds out his favorite aunt has deserted him again."

"I'll be his favorite aunt for the weekend," Olivia said with a laugh. "You want to see him, right?"

"Right."

"And I thought you were going to start doing more of what you want."

"I am."

"So go, Rebecca. Go now."

Rebecca sat where she was for another few seconds, trying to contain the tidal wave of feelings inside her.

Then she jumped out of her seat and ran to her room to pack a bag.

She was in her car and on her way to Phil in less than thirty minutes.

Fourteen

At almost seven, Phil was back on the Eastern Shore, parking his bike on the side of the building, stopping in to make sure everything was fine with the shop, and then walking into the restaurant to let Larry know he'd returned.

Stella didn't work the bar on Friday evenings, so Max was there tonight, filling up drinks quickly and laughing about what someone had said. Phil waved to him as he passed the bar on the way to the kitchen.

Larry never had time for small talk at dinnertime, but he glanced up from the piece of trout he was plating, gave Phil a quick look, and asked, "Everything good?"

"Everything's good."

Larry nodded and went back to his work.

Phil was chuckling as he left.

Maybe it was ridiculous since he and Rebecca hadn't ridden off into the sunset, but he was happy.

Happy, relieved, and pleased with what he'd done.

It felt like he'd done something good, and he had hope for the future. Rebecca hadn't rejected him. She wasn't angry or expecting him to jump through a bunch of hoops. She needed time, and he understood that.

Time he could do.

He wasn't going to mess things up with her again.

He went to the shop to get his fishing rod and tackle bag, and then he headed out to the pier. There were a lot of people out and about tonight—a Friday evening in the summer. The parking lot of the restaurant was full and so was the public beach parking.

He'd just stepped onto the pier when someone called out from behind him.

He turned at the familiar female voice and saw Stella getting out of her old Cadillac, which she'd pulled over on the side of the road.

"Why are you back already?" Stella asked, speaking loudly to be heard over the distance as she hurried over to where he was standing. "She didn't forgive you after all?"

"She did," Phil said when she'd reached him. "She did forgive me. It's good."

"Then why are you here and not with her?"

"I needed to work tomorrow, and we're going to take it slow."

"Why are you taking it slow? You're in love with her, aren't you?" Stella's eyes were wide and knowing.

"Yeah." Phil glanced away. "But it's been twice now that I've left her high and dry. She's trying to make sure this is right for her. I don't want to take it slow, but she does. So we will. As long as she wants it."

Stella's face softened, and she reached out to squeeze his arm. "You're a good one. You know that, right? I've always seen it."

Phil cleared his throat, feeling ridiculously self-conscious. "I haven't always been good."

"Well, you're good now. Your girl is going to see it too. I don't think it'll take very—" She broke off just then, her face changing dramatically into surprise and pleasure and amazement, like she'd seen some sort of miracle over his shoulder.

Bewildered, Phil turned to see what had distracted her.

What he saw was a small blue sedan, which had pulled onto the side of the road behind Stella's Cadillac. Neither vehicle was parked legally.

Then Phil saw who was getting out of the sedan. She was small and pretty and wearing a ponytail and beaming as she started to run toward him.

Rebecca.

His mind wasn't working. He wasn't sure how she could have possibly gotten here since he'd left her a few hours ago at Holiday Acres.

She was supposed to still be there. He was going to call her this evening.

She wasn't supposed to be here. At the pier. Running toward him like her life depended on it.

But she was here, and she'd nearly reached him now.

He dropped his bag and his rod just in time to catch her as she launched herself at him. The momentum spun them both around, and he wrapped his arms around her. She was laughing or crying or maybe both at once.

"Wh—" He couldn't get the whole word out. He buried his face in her neck.

"I'm sure," she burst out, pulling away so she could look up at his face. "I'm sure."

He blinked. "You're…"

"Sure." She was smiling so fully it was shining out of her, but her expression momentarily faltered. "I mean, if you still want—"

"Oh my God, baby." He pulled her into another hug so tightly he was shaking with it. "Of course I still want it. I thought it was too soon."

"It was this morning. But it's not now. I'm sure. I want to be with you. Only you. For as long as you'll have me."

"I've never wanted anyone else." He was still hugging her, rocking her just slightly. His mind was finally starting to catch up, and it was almost too much. Too much emotion for him to contain.

"Well, kiss her, dummy!" That was Stella, who was still standing nearby. "This is your big moment."

Phil gave her a wry look and then turned back to Rebecca, who'd withdrawn slightly, although her arms were still wrapped around his neck.

Then he kissed her, and she kissed him back, and it was eager and clumsy and real.

Stella and everyone else on the pier started clapping, but Phil didn't even care.

Rebecca was blushing and smiling when they finally broke the kiss. She dropped her eyelashes. She'd never liked to be the center of attention.

"Should we go somewhere to talk?" Phil asked. "Somewhere a little more private?"

"Don't you need to fish? To work, I mean?"

"I'll just tell Mary I'm leaving. I can take the evening off."

Rebecca finally let him go. She had to brush away a tear. "Okay. Private sounds good to me."

~

It took them a few minutes to make their escape since they had to accept the well-wishes of Stella and some of the other locals who were hanging out on the pier. But eventually Phil was able to let Mary know he was heading out for the evening. Then he got into Rebecca's car with her, and they drove to his place.

When she parked the car behind his truck, he said, "It's not like your vacation house. Just to warn you."

"I'm sure it's fine. I really don't care."

So Phil showed her up to his run-down studio, and she laughed at the Spartan design but didn't seem particularly put off by anything. He got them both a cold beer, and they went to sit out on his roof deck, which had the best view of the bay.

The evening was humid and still hot, but there was a good breeze from this vantage point, so it wasn't unpleasant.

Phil felt good, and Rebecca was smiling. He didn't have a complaint in the world.

"You must have left just an hour or so after me," he said, taking a swallow of his beer.

"I did. I saw that contract you'd signed—and hadn't even told me about—and I just... knew."

He hadn't seen Rebecca smiling like this since she'd been a teenager, as if all the sunshine in the world was concentrated in her heart and bursting out.

It made him strangely proud. "I didn't sign it as some sort of gesture. Or maybe it was a gesture but not for you. For *me*. I wanted to really... resolve things."

"I know you did. I know why you signed it and why you didn't make a big deal about it. And that's how I knew for sure. Because you meant it. Whether or not we were together, you meant it."

He nodded. "I do mean it. But I do really want us to be together."

"I want that too. I think we can make it work. And I want it to be for real. As real as... as we can make it."

He reached over to take her hand. "I want that too."

They sat like that for a couple of minutes, drinking their beer, holding hands, staring at the sea. And Phil wondered if he'd ever been so perfectly, purely happy in his life.

Responding to this thought, he said, "I can move back home, if that's what you want. I don't want to leave Larry in the lurch, but I'm sure I can work something out. I can move home—or to Richmond while you're in cooking school there—or whatever works best. I'll give up anything I need to give up to make things work with you."

"I don't want you to give up things you love, Phil. And I'm not sure either of us will need to give up everything. I was thinking while I was driving here about how it might work, and I have an idea."

"Yeah?" That was something he hadn't expected, and he wasn't sure how he'd be able to handle any more good news.

He'd fully prepared to give up his fishing shop in order to be with Rebecca. He'd assumed it was a necessary sacrifice, and he hadn't begrudged it at all.

"Yeah. You were saying there's hardly anything for you to do in the fall and winter here, and of course the fall and winter is when we're busiest at Holiday Acres and when they'll need my help the most. So I was thinking..."

"Shit," Phil breathed. "You want to split our time?"

"Maybe. If you think it would work. Doesn't it make sense? We could spend half the year here and the other half at Holiday Acres. And then all we'd be missing is the off-seasons of both places. Do you think Larry would go for that?"

"I'm sure he would. I'm sure he would. Shit, that might just work." Phil was shaking his head, amazed that such an obvious solution had never occurred to him.

But then he'd never really been looking for solutions. He'd just been running away.

"So you want to try that?" Rebecca asked, her eyes full of excitement. "I know my sisters would be fine with it. They keep telling me I can leave for good if I want to, but I do love Holiday Acres and I want to stay involved if I can. But I want you to hold on to your life too, and I do really love it here." She paused and then flashed him a quick smile. "But if we're going to be here several months a year, then maybe we could find a slightly nicer place than this to live in."

Phil burst into laughter. "I'm sure we could." He reached out again to take her hand. "So you don't have any doubts, baby?"

"No doubts. No doubts at all."

"So we can... really start planning our future?"

"Definitely."

"And it's okay to tell you I love you?"

Her breath hitched, and her hand jerked in his grip just slightly. Then she gave him a wobbly smile. "It's okay with me since I love you too."

He stifled a groan and leaned over to kiss her.

For a moment he was drowning in her, but it wasn't the kind of drowning that would kill him.

It was the kind that would teach him to swim.

~

They stayed on the roof, talking and making plans for a couple of hours. By then it was dark and they were hungry, so they fixed a simple dinner and ate it at Phil's tiny table.

Rebecca had brought an overnight bag with her, and she took a shower before she got ready for bed. Then Phil took a quick one and came out wearing just his underwear to find that Rebecca was waiting for him in bed.

She was smiling at him from the pillow, and his heart gave a ridiculous gallop.

It wasn't just excitement—although it certainly was that. It was more than that. It was emotion so deep Phil hadn't thought he was capable of it anymore.

He crawled into bed beside her and rolled over to kiss her.

They kissed for a long time before he started to stroke her body. He took off her little gown and kissed her all over until she was squirming and whimpering. She was openly eager, clawing at his back and tugging on his hair and trying to wrap her legs around him, and her responsiveness was intoxicating.

"Phil, I'm ready any time," she said at last.

His mouth was working on one of her breasts, teasing her nipple until she couldn't lie still. "I know you are, baby. But this is for you."

"It's for both of us."

"It's for both of us," he agreed, giving her a tug with his teeth that made her cry out loudly. "Nothing in the world is better than making you come."

"Oh God, Phil," she gasped, arching up dramatically as he felt between her legs. "You're gonna kill me before the end of this."

"Maybe. But you're going to enjoy the end." He was smiling as he felt how hot and wet she was. He couldn't believe his sweet, quiet, little Rebecca could get so turned on, could lose all her inhibitions this way.

He slid a finger inside her and rubbed her inner walls. They clenched around him hard, and Rebecca cried out loudly.

"That's right, baby," he murmured since he knew she loved when he talked her through it. "I can feel how much you want this."

She clenched around him again, biting her lower lip and tossing her head on the pillow.

He lowered his mouth to her breast again and suckled as he joined the finger with another and moved them hard and fast.

She was coming apart quickly, shaking and whimpering and reaching out to clutch at the bedding. She was babbling out pleas for him to make her come, how much she needed it, how only he could give it her.

Phil's erection was a throbbing presence at his groin, but nothing in the world was going to distract him from this, from giving Rebecca everything she needed. He pumped his fingers hard and sucked hard on her breast.

She sobbed out an orgasm, writhing beneath him as she rode out the spasms. Her channel clamped down around his fingers so hard it threatened to push him out. She was limp and gasping and smiling when he'd soothed her through the last of the contractions.

He found her lips and kissed her softly. "All for you."

"All for us."

He smiled against her lips. "All for us."

She wrapped one arm around him and held him down to deepen the kiss. And as they kissed, she freed his erection from his underwear with the other hand. He fumbled to line himself up at her entrance, and she wrapped her legs around him as he sank inside her.

She was so hot and wet and tight without the condom. She was so everything. All he'd ever dreamed of. His body was moving of its own accord, thrusting, rocking, moving with hers, taking what he needed.

What both of them needed.

She was with him all the way, gasping and making pretty little grunts as things started to feel good for her. He could feel the tension building in her body, even as it was building in his. He moved harder, more urgently, starting to grunt loudly as the pleasure built up.

"Phil," she gasped. "Phil, I'm gonna come again."

"Yes. Yes, baby. Oh yes." He was fucking her so hard now the bed was shaking, her soft body was shaking, everything was shaking. He could feel her tightening around him.

Then she was crying out as an orgasm shuddered through her, and Phil's vision whited out with pleasure as the last thread of his control finally snapped.

He roared as he came, pushing into her clumsily, feeling the release well up and burst out as he came inside her.

He was hot and exhausted and completely sated as he collapsed on top of her when he'd given her everything he had. She stroked his hair and his back. Her legs were still wrapped around him. His whole body was softening.

He loved her, and she was his.

"I love you, Phil," she said hoarsely against his ear.

"I love you too, baby. So much."

"So much."

"I've loved you since you were sixteen years old."

"Not that long."

"Yes, that long. You're the only woman I ever loved. And I think I loved you all the time we were apart. I just was afraid to let myself. But I'm not afraid now."

"I'm not afraid either. I'm going to start taking what I want, and the first thing I want is you."

"Then you have me." He made himself roll off her since he knew he'd start getting heavy. But he kept his head turned to meet her eyes. "For as long as you want me, you have me."

"I'm pretty sure I'm going to want you forever."

"Forever sounds about right to me."

~

They went to sleep shortly afterward, and Phil woke up the next morning, happier than he could ever remember being.

They drank coffee and then made love again, and then Rebecca went with him to the pier at seven to fish.

She didn't fish the whole time. She walked around after a while and bought them a couple of donuts. But she was clearly serious about learning to fish—more serious than she'd been before.

And it meant something to Phil.

It meant she cared about what was important to him.

And so it was right and fitting and perfectly symbolic when, at 9:43 that morning, she caught her first fish.

They took a picture and then let it go, and Rebecca was beaming with excitement the whole time.

Phil might have been beaming a little bit too.

Epilogue

Four months later, it was one week before Christmas, and Phil and Rebecca were back at Holiday Acres.

Rebecca had been in cooking school for two months, and she had two more months to go after Christmas, so they hadn't been able to help out at Holiday Acres this year as much as she would have wanted to. But everyone insisted that cooking school was more important, and she was having such a good time she had to agree.

But she and Phil were going to spend the next two weeks at home, and she was incredibly happy about that.

She'd missed her sisters and Tommy. And the staff. And even Russ and his acerbic attitude.

Plus it was Christmas, and that always made her happy.

At the moment, the family was gathered in their private living room in the upper floor of the farmhouse. There was a fire blazing in the fireplace, and they were eating snacks she'd made and drinking hot cider and spiced wine. Russ was here, and even Scott had deigned to come after Phil had asked him four different times. Olivia wasn't happy about Scott's presence. She kept shooting him cool, resentful looks which Scott kept smugly ignoring. But otherwise everyone was happy and in a festive mood.

Things were better, Rebecca realized as she looked around the room from her seat near the fire. It felt like family. Not like the broken remnants that had been left of their families seven years ago.

It was proof that healing was possible. Hard and long and sometimes wrenching—but possible.

Phil had been talking to his brother across the room, but now he came over and scooted her over so he could fit in the seat beside her. It was snug and overly warm, but she had no complaints in the world.

She leaned against his familiar body. "Is Scott doing okay?"

"He's okay, I think. I think it actually helps that Olivia doesn't like him. It gives him something to think about rather than feeling uncomfortable being here." Phil had wrapped an arm around her, and he squeezed her with it as he nestled against him.

"Good. I hope he hangs out with us a little more. I don't like us holding on to all that resentment."

"I don't like it either. I still can't get Kent out of his cabin, but I'll keep trying."

Rebecca exhaled and relaxed against him. She felt so good, so warm, so incredibly pleased with the world. It was so hard to remember who she'd been six months ago.

They sat together for a few minutes, looking around at their families. Then Phil cleared his throat and said, "I have something for you."

She glanced up at his face. "What do you have?"

His expression was oddly stiff as he stuck his hand in his pocket and pulled out of a wad of blue fabric. "I was going to wait until Christmas, but I can't wait anymore. I've always thought that hoping for something good would mean I'd end up getting crushed, but I don't think that anymore. I want something good, and I don't want to wait for it."

She had no idea what he was talking about, but she recognized the fabric in his hand. "Hey, that's my scarf. I wondered what had happened to it."

"I kept it."

"You did?"

"Yeah. But I'm giving it back now."

She was bewildered by the urgency in his expression, but she accepted the scarf he handed her. It was soft and thin, and through the fabric she felt that there was something inside the folds.

She opened it to discover a pretty ring in the fabric. A gold band. An emerald-cut diamond solitaire.

She stiffened dramatically, her breath caught in her throat.

"I was going to wait until Christmas," Phil said again. "But I can't wait anymore."

She kept staring down at the ring.

"Rebecca," he murmured. "Will you marry me?"

Her eyes blurred over. Her heart was so big it constricted her chest. She opened her mouth to respond but couldn't say anything.

"Is that a yes?" he prompted, his expression flickering slightly.

"Yes!" she burst out, far too loudly for a crowded room. "Yes!"

She clenched her fist around the ring and scarf and threw her arms around him.

The others in the room heard her answer, and it didn't take them long to figure out what had just happened in the chair by the fire. So the private moment wasn't exactly private.

But Rebecca and Phil were too happy to care.

About Noelle Adams

Noelle handwrote her first romance novel in a spiral-bound notebook when she was twelve, and she hasn't stopped writing since. She has lived in eight different states and currently resides in Virginia, where she writes full time, reads any book she can get her hands on, and offers tribute to a very spoiled cocker spaniel.

She loves travel, art, history, and ice cream. After spending far too many years of her life in graduate school, she has decided to reorient her priorities and focus on writing contemporary romances. For more information, please check out her website: noelle-adams.com.

Books by Noelle Adams

Holiday Acres

      Stranded on the Beach
      Stranded in the Snow
      Stranded in the Woods
      Stranded for Christmas

Trophy Husbands

      Part-Time Husband
      Practice Husband
      Packaged Husband

The Loft Series

Living with Her One-Night Stand
Living with Her Ex-Boyfriend
Living with Her Fake Fiancé

One Fairy Tale Wedding Series
Unguarded
Untouched
Unveiled

Tea for Two Series
Falling for her Brother's Best Friend
Winning her Brother's Best Friend
Seducing her Brother's Best Friend

Balm in Gilead Series
Relinquish
Surrender
Retreat

Rothman Royals Series
A Princess Next Door
A Princess for a Bride
A Princess in Waiting
Christmas with a Prince

Preston's Mill Series (co-written with Samantha Chase)
Roommating
Speed Dating
Procreating

Eden Manor Series
One Week with her Rival

One Week with her (Ex) Stepbrother
One Week with her Husband
Christmas at Eden Manor

Beaufort Brides Series
Hired Bride
Substitute Bride
Accidental Bride

Heirs of Damon Series
Seducing the Enemy
Playing the Playboy
Engaging the Boss
Stripping the Billionaire

Willow Park Series
Married for Christmas
A Baby for Easter
A Family for Christmas
Reconciled for Easter
Home for Christmas

One Night Novellas
One Night with her Best Friend
One Night in the Ice Storm
One Night with her Bodyguard
One Night with her Boss
One Night with her Roommate
One Night with the Best Man

The Protectors Series (co-written with Samantha Chase)
Protecting his Best Friend's Sister

Protecting the Enemy
Protecting the Girl Next Door
Protecting the Movie Star

Standalones
A Negotiated Marriage
Listed
Bittersweet
Missing
Revival
Holiday Heat
Salvation
Excavated
Overexposed
Road Tripping
Chasing Jane
Late Fall
Fooling Around
Married by Contract
Trophy Wife
Bay Song
Her Reluctant Billionaire
Second Best

Made in the USA
Middletown, DE
22 October 2018